scarborough

scarbo

rough

Catherine Hernandez

Arsenal Pulp Press
Vancouver

ARSENAL PULP PRESS
Suite 202 – 211 East Georgia St.
Vancouver, BC V6A 1Z6
Canada
arsenalpulp.com

The publisher gratefully acknowledges the support of the Canada Council for the Arts and
the British Columbia Arts Council for its publishing program, and the Government of Canada (through the Canada Book Fund) and the Government of British Columbia (through the
Book Publishing Tax Credit Program) for its publishing activities.

This is a work of fiction. Any resemblance of characters to persons either living or deceased is
purely coincidental.

Cover and text design by Oliver McPartlin
Cover photo by Matthew Henry
Back cover photo by WanderingToronto
Edited by Robyn So

Printed and bound in Canada

Library and Archives Canada Cataloguing in Publication:
Hernandez, Catherine, 1977-, author
    Scarborough / Catherine Hernandez.

Issued in print and electronic formats.
ISBN 978-1-55152-677-5 (softcover).--ISBN 978-1-55152-678-2 (HTML).

    I. Title.

PS8615.E75S23 2017   C813'.6   C2017-901407-2
                                             C2017-901408-0

I was fifteen. You were four.
I taught you drama in a Scarborough community centre.
You were surviving neglect.
Wherever you are, I hope you are safe
and know I loved you enough to write you this book.

To all the Scarborough girls
who dreamt of embraces
who, like my sister and so many
only found gold in his teeth but not in his heart
felt the brass on his knuckles
but not the tender caress of his palm
who never felt the fall of rain
but rejoiced in the fall of freshly ironed, blood-stained bills
To all my east end women
who lick the pastry of beef patties from between their teeth
and walk in rhythm to the music from each store in the strip mall
who know the song of new nails
the acrylics biting into our hands as we spin and make the pole
squeak the squeal of money earned
To all of my sisters who have pushed powder for baby formula
riding the wave of how much and how come and how long and how
will we
and feeling the cold tile of Warden Station against our fingertips and
against the back of our thighs
To all the young mothers who carry the weight of twenty-dollar
strollers aboard the bus to their next wish
praying each time we peek at the stillness of the water between coats
and between stops
bowing our heads low when the po pass
singing echoes through graffiti-kissed tunnels
guarding our spliffs from the harsh wind, dandelions by our hearts
I see you.

LAURA

I am standing just close enough to Mommy, until she begins to speak to me. I don't understand what she's saying, but I know better than to ask her to say it again.

She puts two plastic bags on the floor. She opens them up the way you open up socks so your foot can fit in. They look like two circles. I watch.

Mommy begins putting things into the circles. Whatever she can reach with her arms. Her hair is over her eyes, and I don't know if she can even see what she's reaching for. I want to help her, but I don't know why she's doing this.

"You're going to your dad's."

I look up to the wall behind Mommy's head, to see if I can picture his face in my mind, but I can't remember it. I'm not sure if I'm excited. Maybe Daddy has snacks.

"Get all your things. We're leaving."

I see Mommy has packed a bag, too. I run to my Mama Duck paper cut-outs on the windowsill. I gather Mama Duck and all her ducklings into my hand and carefully walk to the two plastic bag circles. Mommy slaps my hands, and I watch the yellow paper cut-outs fall to the floor.

"Not those. Stop it! Go get your clothes."

I search the floor for my clothes. But all I can see are the yellow paper cut-outs of Mama Duck and her babies. What will they do without me?

Mommy slaps the back of my head, and my cheeks get hot.

"Get your fucking clothes."

I find my underwear in the hamper where I put it to get clean. I find my leggings under the kitchen table where I played house, then fell asleep. I find two shirts in the tub, where I rinsed them. They are still kind of damp. Mommy says there's no time to dry them.

I put the clothes into the plastic bag circles. Mommy rolls them back out and up so they hold things. She points to my jacket. I place it upside down on the floor like I always do, because it's easier to put on. I put my arms into the arm holes and flip it over my head. One, two, flipperoo. Mommy helps me with the zipper.

"Hurry the hell up."

She takes the plastic bags and ties one to each of my wrists. She makes fists of my hands around the handles. She kneels in front of me and wipes her hair from her face so that I can see her eyes. I haven't seen her eyes in a long time.

"Do not let go of these, got it?" I nod. "We have to be like little mice, Laura. When we leave, we have to whisper until we're outside. You understand?" I nod.

She gets her big bag and puts it on her shoulder. It looks heavy. Maybe Daddy is far away.

Mommy looks back into the apartment and turns off the lights. We open the door. Mommy puts her finger to her mouth to remind me to be quiet.

We step over all the coloured paper that has been left outside our door. Mommy lifts her feet up and down softly, like she's creeping up behind someone.

I see her reach into her pocket, and she pulls out a silver key. She places it on a table inside the apartment, then closes the door silently.

Across the hall, Mrs Kamal opens her door. Mommy freezes. Mrs Kamal looks at me, then looks at Mommy. They stare at each other for a long time. Mr Kamal calls from inside. Mrs Kamal says something back to him, then reaches for a pair of boots she left to dry in the hallway. I want to tell her so badly that I am going to see my daddy. That he is going to have snacks. And to tell her thank you. But Mrs Kamal is looking down at the boots in her hand, pretending she can't see us.

We take the back stairwell down to the rear door. It is almost night. The wind rushes through the leaves of the trees, and it sounds like they're clapping at me. Like the wind is saying something. I want to stay and listen, but Mommy brings my hood up over my ears.

"Come on," she says. "We're going for a ride."

Ontario Reads Literacy Program
221 Harbord Square
Toronto, Ontario

June 6, 2011

Ms Hina Hassani
242 Celeste Court
Toronto, Ontario

Dear Hina,

We are pleased to offer you the position of Program Facilitator at the Rouge Hill Public School location of the Ontario Reads Literacy Program. It was a unanimous decision by the board members, based on the resounding success of the Toronto Young Fathers in Action Centre in Rexdale, under your guidance. This position will commence on August 20, 2011, to allow you to prepare for the beginning of the school year on September 6, 2011.

As you are well aware, the Ontario Reads Literacy Program is a provincial initiative to prepare children for scholastic success and to encourage families to be a part of their children's learning by

- fostering and cultivating skills in literacy and numeracy through stories, music, reading, and playing;
- teaching caregivers and parents ways to engage in their children's learning through song, dance, and basic play;
- providing a lending library of books in different languages so parents can read to their children in their first language;

- sharing amongst community members songs and stories of different cultures during storytime;
- building community and camaraderie through clothing, book, and food exchanges;
- spending time with other children and their families;
- providing space to be active and access to a wide variety of toys that low-income families may not otherwise have;
- linking families with appropriate community resources for special needs, health, and other related services;
- promoting healthy eating with daily provisions of snacks;
- giving children the opportunity to adjust to scholastic life by establishing locations within local schools.

As a facilitator at the Rouge Hill Public School location, you will work closely with children from infants up to ten years of age. You will be joining a league of facilitators who head 203 centres located across the province and who uphold the standards by which the Ontario Reads Literacy Program prepares children for scholastic success while building community.

That said, each location is vastly different. While facilitators are expected to adhere to operation policies, factors such as socioeconomic barriers and concentrations of various cultures will give each centre its own energy. As you know, outreach takes time and trust. In time, you will most certainly build relationships and familiarize yourself with your community's members, elders, and children. We are confident, given your experience at the Rexdale Toronto Young Fathers in Action Centre, that you possess the skills to outreach effectively to the Kingston/Galloway area of Scarborough.

Please find enclosed our welcome package, including a staff directory, union guidelines, budget allocation sheets, and attendance/registration forms.

Congratulations, and welcome to our team.

Sincerely,
Geraldine McDonough
Executive Director, Ontario Reads Literacy Program

PART ONE

FALL

The black flies have come early this year and have bitten away all the beachcombers along the mouth of the Rouge River. Grandfather Heron watches amongst the reeds before silently flying to his hiding place.

At the corner of Lawson and Centennial Roads
With shadows long from an early sunset, the gals at the Pampered Paws nail salon close up shop. It has been a long day of thirty-dollar pedicures.

At Kennedy Station
Just a month ago, this joint was full of festivalgoers in their Caribana finery heading downtown. Now the wind blows a fierce warning of a dark season to come.

SYLVIE

Mama forced me into double-time walking, which I didn't mind because I was wearing my favourite dark brown corduroys. She said each one of her steps equalled two of mine, which meant I had to walk twice as fast. Mama wanted to make it to the shelter before five o'clock so that she could have the kitchen in peace. She had scored a can of beef gravy and a box of Hamburger Helper at the food bank, but in order to brown the meat properly she had to call dibs on the better stovetop and the better frying pan before Mrs Abdul "took over the whole goddamn show."

I couldn't hear much of Mama's complaining and nagging over the vrip, vrip, vrip of my corduroy inner thighs, and that suited me just fine. I'm kind of tired of listening to her talk about Johnny this and Johnny that. See, at first it seemed my little brother was gifted, being such a good climber and so good at picking locks, undoing zippers, clicking buckles in and out, running down the hallway. But when Mama noticed he did all of this to the tune of his constant humming, she knew she had to bring him to the walk-in clinic.

"Can I have his health card, please?" the receptionist asked. Mama nudged me and pointed to her bulky black purse under Johnny's stroller. I grabbed it and tried to lift it to her. It sure was heavy.

"Thank you, sweet girl." Mama patted me on the head. While we waited for the receptionist to check Johnny's health card, I hung on the counter like a monkey. "Get your hands off the counter, you silly goose!" I did what I was told, having gone from a sweet girl to a silly goose with one mistake.

The receptionist handed Mama a clipboard with a form on it. "Go ahead and have a seat. Just fill this out, and hand it to me when you're done." She suddenly turned to a shirtless man coming out of a room, the sounds of a toilet flushing behind him. He was zipping up his jeans. Her lips pursed. We stood frozen, not knowing what to do.

"Did you speak to the doctor yet, nurse?"

"Yes. And he says he cannot give you a prescription for that. Narcotics are not prescribed here."

"You know what? I'm here to get medication for my anxiety, okay!?" He began to pace the waiting room. "And you not giving me what I want is giving me more anxiety!"

"Sir. I am going to need you to calm down." The receptionist put her hand on the desk phone, like a threat.

He had a look on his face, like he knew something clever. Like he knew he was about to put all his cards down playing Go Fish. "What you're doing is against the hypothetical oath! I'm going to call my lawyers right now!" He dug into his pockets and found his cellphone.

"Sir! There are no cellphones allowed in the clinic."

He threw his hands into the air. "Aw, fuck! Fuck you all." He slammed the door as he left.

We took our place in the U-shaped seating area.

"See, Mama? I told you I shouldn't have come. Now I've missed Indian Taco Day at school."

"Oh, enough! You don't understand how tricky it is, Sylvie," Mama explained. "We gotta get in the clinic between noon and four to avoid the lineups. No fry bread for you right now, but you can wait until next time. Jeez." She nudged me and pointed at a copy of *Chatelaine* magazine sitting on the coffee table. I fetched it for her. She patted me on the head. "Thanks, sweet girl." I shook my head.

We sat in that waiting room for two whole hours. I watched a boy crawl underneath the coffee table and listened to him cough like he was choking on worms.

"Parker, sit down," said his mom in a weak voice. "Parker? Parker, please. Come on. Can you sit down for me?" The kid kept crawling on the filthy floor.

Mama looked at me and rolled her eyes. She could write a book on parenting based on her eye rolls.

"Parker? Why don't you sit down and have something to drink?" The mom searched her diaper bag and pulled out a bottle of Grape-C Plus. She shook it toward him like he was a cat looking at a treat. "Come on. Sit down. Please? Parker?"

Mama stomped her foot to get rid of her frustration. This parenting book she was writing in her head was getting awfully thick.

Parker finally came out from under the table, sat, and downed the pop. Then he was done sitting, so hopped up on sugar that he jumped from chair to chair and ripped out pages from outdated copies of *Reader's Digest* issues piled around the seating area.

"Uh-oh. That's not nice, Parker. No thank you. We don't do that. Why don't you sit down and have a chocolate bar?"

It was frustrating to watch—but our frustration was only just beginning.

"I think he's got a problem," Mama said to the doctor when we were finally called in.

His eyes never left his prescription pad as he avoided eye contact with the Native woman before him—her hair, like brushed-out wool, hanging to her hips and framing her slightly bucked teeth, her accent as undulating as the East Coast landscape she came from.

"He's three, but he doesn't say much, and the rest of the time, he's humming to himself."

"Lots of kids sing to themselves, Miss Beaudoin."

"You don't understand. He doesn't even look you in the eye when you're talking to him. He'll put anything in his mouth. I even threw a ball at him so's I could see his reaction. He didn't even raise his arms to protect his face. It was a soft ball, eh. Nothing hard, mind you. I just know there's something wrong."

It was too painful to watch my mother being ignored, so I took some tongue depressors from the counter and began making a fort with them. Johnny, of course, smashed my creation. Mama pried the sticks from Johnny's hands and put them back on the counter. The doctor eyed the dirty tongue depressors and sighed.

Someone knocked on the door, and the doctor wheeled his stool toward it. He opened the door just a crack and began whispering to the receptionist on the other side.

"He's back, doctor."

"Well, what did you tell him?"

"What I told him last time. That we don't prescribe narcotics."

"And?"

"He's threatening to sue us."

"He can't sue us for not doling out oxycodone at a walk-in clinic."

"But he's getting aggressive with me. I'm pretty sure he's going to attack me."

"Fine. I'll be out in a second."

The doctor turned back to Mama and sighed.

"Let's just say something is wrong with Johnny. What do you achieve then?" He cracked his knuckles and rubbed his hands together.

Mama knew this was a trick question.

"Well ... I guess then we can find the right support for him."

"It's not like once you get a diagnosis for a learning disability, some specialist waves a magic wand and he'll be healed, Miss Beaudoin. It's a lot of work. And from what I understand of your situation, this is the least of your worries."

Mama's cheeks flushed. She gently pried the otoscope from Johnny's hands and placed it back in its wall holder.

"My advice is to deal with one thing at a time." The doctor was already standing with one hand on the doorknob. "Truth is, next year he'll be in school. You can trust that a teacher will bring it up if there's a problem. And if there is a problem, a specialist will visit the school for you."

"Not at this school. This school doesn't have the time or money, doctor."

"Miss Beaudoin." He took his glasses off. "I know you mentioned you're at the Galloway Shelter. I can't imagine how hard it is to deal with these challenges in such small quarters. But once your housing is settled and Johnny is a bit older, maybe then we can talk about assessments. There's a lot of back and forth with specialists. A lot of booking appointments, phone calls, trips across town. Think about dealing with all of that in addition to what you're dealing with now. Besides, I have a strong feeling he's just a bit behind. Nothing to worry about."

The entire time Mama begged the fool for a referral, I thought how unfair it was that I was missing Rouge Hill Public School's Native Taco Day. And for nothing. I pictured my grade three classmates in line in the gym, the smell of chili powder and fry bread in the air. I could see the dollops of sour cream being dropped on each of the tacos, and the shreds of cheese. Mrs Falls, with her hair net and all, would have let me into the line without a toonie, giving me a knowing wink. I could have been there. Instead, I was rushing out of a stupid walk-in clinic, hoping to catch the Number 86 Scarborough so we could be back at the shelter before five.

At least I got to imagine the sensation of Hamburger Helper with extra gravy filling my tummy. That's what went through my mind the entire bus ride home while I elbowed Johnny's sleeping head off of my shoulders over and over again like a yo-yo.

My earnest double-time walking was rewarded by the satisfying *shhhhh plop* of the noodles falling into the boiling water. I was asked to place the cardboard box in the recycling with the other boxes of food bank fare. All the labels looked back at me: bowls of hearty meals, steaming and smiling; a family far away who would rather have something fresh and fancy; a family far away wanting to teach their kids something about charity.

"But what about the directions?" I asked.

"I don't need directions for Hamburger Helper. I've had enough of it in my lifetime," Mama said before ripping open the cheese sauce packet. A cloud of crayon orange revealed ribbons of sunlight in the shelter kitchen. We giggled, it was so pretty.

That's when we saw Mrs Abdul by the door, giving my mama cut-eye when she saw how perfect our timing was. This made me and Mama giggle even more.

The next morning, dust from the bottom of the cereal box got caught in my eyes. I went to school squinting one eye and then the other, just so I wouldn't bump into anything. Mama always warned me not to act stupid, otherwise the school counsellor would bring me to her office. This counsellor, Mrs Rhodes, likes to collect brown-people things and put them up on her wall. Things like coolie hats, dashikis, masks. Next to these brown-people things are pictures of her and her sunburnt children wearing the coolie hats, dashikis, and masks. I really wanted to play with the tea set she got from Japan, but everyone warned me. Indian kids who go into that office with cereal dust in their eyes are referred to an eye doctor who diagnoses eye disease and gives you a prescription, which your parents can't afford, and the next thing you know, Children's Aid is all up in your parents' business wondering why they can't afford any medicated drops for their children's busted-up eyes. You walk in there a kid; you walk out of there a ward of the state. You can't trust them, coolie hat or no coolie hat.

I crept past Mrs Rhodes' office and into my classroom, pretending everything was right as rain. My new morning ritual involved taking my coat and backpack off right quick, hanging everything up as fast as lightning, and running like the wind to my desk. I imagined this would make it difficult for everyone in class to see I was wearing the same corduroys as yesterday. Mama works hard to ensure that we are as clean as possible, but with only three sets of clothes, National Thrift being so very far away, and a washing machine that is broken when it isn't being hogged by Mrs Abdul, it sometimes means turning my underwear inside out. It doesn't help that Johnny is in a phase where he eats anything off the floor. This week he really enjoyed eating markers. He barfed Crimson Red and Sky Blue all over his jacket—twice. Mama was so tired.

One day, just after dinner, Mama had an emergency. It was the type of emergency where she was opening drawers randomly, searching for things, and begging us not to ask her any more questions. She took me by the wrist, so I knew something was really wrong. Mama always holds me by the hand, our fingers intertwined, unless there is a missing piece of the puzzle, or the pieces are fitting together all wrong. These wrong things happen often, which is why I was familiar with the feeling. These wrong things explain the Why Here and the Why Now. But they never explain the Where To or the How Will We.

She frantically knocked on 215, the door of Mr George down the hall. He was Ojibwa and the only person that Mama both trusted and found available most times. Although Slutty Christy was super nice, Mama hated people who smoked in their room despite being steps from the shelter's back entrance. It was against the rules, and Christy just didn't care. At least Mr George was one of us and as harmless as an aloe plant.

Mr George opened the door and nodded. I wasn't sure if he was agreeing to take me for a while, or if it was the Parkinson's. Either way, Mama pulled me inside and plopped me atop his couch, seated close enough to him to have a perfect view of the gaping hole at his throat. It was a warning to me, Mama said. Since the minute he was born, Mr George was smoking Rez cigarettes like it was his job. Those cigarettes burned right through him, making a doorway to his Adam's apple. I often sit on his couch for hours watching his strange throat hole move around like a jelly's mouth while he enjoys his afternoon of game shows on his old TV.

By the time Mama came to pick me up, I was asleep in Mr George's arms, hearing the prizes being announced on *Wheel of Fortune* somewhere far away in my dreams.

I had never really heard Mr George speak in full sentences before, and now he was mumbling something to Mama.

"I'm so sorry it took so long," Mama said, flustered. Mr George mumbled something again and Mama responded. "Exactly. Holy shit. The emergency room was packed."

Mr George gave me a pat on the head, and then I could feel Mama picking me up and hoisting me into an upright position, my chin rubbing against the nub of her shoulder. I could have woken up. I could have let her arms rest. But I knew she was sad about something, and this was the best hug I would get from her today. I breathed in the smell of her antiperspirant wafting up her shirt and pretended she was hugging me back.

She expertly placed me into my bed beside Johnny's crib, removed my socks, and put them by the window to air out for tomorrow. Mama tucked me in as she usually did, too tightly, from my toes right up to my chin, fabric gathered around my shoulders, a pillow on either side of me. She kissed my forehead quickly and like a mouse slipped through the door and left it ajar.

I twisted my body toward the action as much as I could despite Mama's swaddling. I watched her leave in a huff. She came back with Johnny in his stroller, sleeping and covered in a blanket. She left the room again, and came back later with Michelle, the shelter supervisor. Dad was sandwiched between them. They inched forward, looking down at their feet and in step with one another, like it was a slow dance. I could tell the weight of Dad was pulling on the long dreads down Michelle's back because her chin was slightly cocked to one side, and her face was twisting.

"Can you lift your foot?" Michelle said.

My dad grunted.

"Marie, can you open the door a bit wider? Perfect. I'm going to hold your elbow right here, Jonathon. Okay, good. We're clear of that door."

"You got the keys, Michelle?"

"In my pocket."

They inched forward. Dad's neck was in a brace. He moaned with his mouth open at every movement.

"Jonathon, Marie. The couch is right behind you. We are going to do this together. Get your bum down right here."

"You think this is a good place to put him?"

"It'll have to do. Okay. Can you get that pillow over there, Marie? No, the bigger one. We can elevate his legs a bit."

One long moan, and my dad was in his spot. It would remain his spot for several weeks.

Michelle turned on the living room lamp to assess the situation. She looked around. My mama and dad were on the couch, tired and hungry, glad for quiet.

"Okay, Marie. This is what I'm going to do. I can see if Mrs Abdul is willing to trade suites with you so that you can be on the ground floor."

"She won't do that. Not for us."

"Well, let's see. Jonathon can barely walk, let alone make it to the elevator, even with two people helping him." Michelle noticed my mama frowning, figuring things out in her head. "Tonight you sleep. Can you promise me that?"

"I'll try." Mama didn't have the strength to laugh, but she managed to give Michelle a goofy smile.

Michelle giggled a little. "At least you get the bed to yourself. Think about that. I even envy you right now." She made that sound she usually makes, sucking air through the gap in her front teeth when she disapproves of something.

Mama smiled weakly. "I think I'll probably sleep here on the couch. I'm too scared."

"I hear you, I hear you." Michelle placed a hand on Mama's

shoulder, which melted at the touch. "You are a good mother and wife, Marie."

Michelle left. There was a long silence, long enough that I dozed off in the pool of quiet, until I heard the cupboards opening and closing.

"Can you at least swallow?" Mama asked Dad as he used his one good arm to try to close his jaw. The soup just dribbled down his chin. "Damn it, Jonathon! What am I gonna do? Open up another can of soup? An imaginary can of soup? We have nothing!"

Dad always looked at the feet of people who were shouting at him when he failed. *Go on, now. Just let it loose and leave me be,* his face seemed to say. Usually when he had this face, he would storm out for long periods of time and come back to Mama crying and begging him to stop visiting the off-track betting place on Ellesmere Road.

This time, though, his big rig had jackknifed on Highway 401 because he was in a rush to get ahead of schedule and ended up falling asleep at the wheel. Now, with all of his injuries, even old Mr George could outrun him. I knew it was a bad time to ask if I could sign his cast, so I continued to pretend to sleep.

Johnny was still in his stroller, dead to the world, sucking his bottom lip.

DAILY REPORT

September 14, 2011

Facilitator: Hina Hassani

Location: Rouge Hill Public School

Attendance:

Parent/Guardian/Caregiver	Children (one per line please)
Lily Chan	Aiden Chan
	Jennifer Chan
Helen McKay	Finnegan Everson
	Sebastian Dennis
	Liam Williams
	Chloe Smith
Amina Mohammed	Waleed Mohammed
Edna Espiritu	Bernard Espiritu
Marie Beaudoin	Sylvie Beaudoin
	Johnny Beaudoin

Notes:

A bit of a slow day today since the centre has just opened within the school. Lots of parents dropping off their kids to school are under the impression this is a daycare and walk past. Some think it is a drop-off space to leave their kids and not a place to play with their preschool children. I'm trying to stay by the door of the centre to greet everyone in the school hallway passing by and to let them know they can come in if they need play-time. Funny enough, since many of the parents in this neighbourhood are English as a Second Language, passing them brochures about the Ontario Reads Literacy Program isn't really catching on. I'm wondering if we could have the brochure translated into other languages. The one thing that's easy to convey is morning and afternoon snack time. As it's a low-income community, parents in this area seem to be quite eager for opportunities to feed their kids.

Today's most popular activities included the sand table, the animal shape sorter, and the magnet magic station. Circle time went very well, despite the quietness at the centre. The kids were full of beans, so I did lots of stand-up songs. Baby Waleed, as usual, thoroughly enjoyed the rainbow song. I make sure I sing it every time he drops in.

There are some great characters who visit me regularly. One elderly woman parks her scooter outside our doors, comes in for a coffee, then leaves. I'm unsure if she has any children who actually attend the school at Rouge Hill. ☺ There's a toddler named Johnny, whom I will be observing closely over the next while for the possibility of learning disabilities. There have been some complaints from some of the caregivers and parents about his behaviour, but I haven't found anything troublesome. I just think he will need more support, and I think the mother, Marie, is a bit overwhelmed. I will observe for now and consider a good time to converse with her as to how I can support her so Johnny can be integrated better into our activities. There are some older kids who attend the centre before class. One of them, Bing, and I have a deal that he can peruse my special closed cabinet of toys as long as he cleans it up. He has very much enjoyed playing with the Little Scientist kit. He has been looking at everything from tissue paper to fingernails under this mini microscope.

Helen, one of our home daycare providers who regularly attends the centre, has asked if she can donate a set of twenty plastic picnic plates so that we don't have to use the coffee filters for plates. I told her I would ask management. Let me know your thoughts.

Weekly supplies requested

2% milk	three bags
Cheerios	two boxes

cucumbers	two large
cheese	marble, one large block
strawberries	one carton (just a pint is fine, since these go bad easily in our tiny fridge!)
high chair	lots of babies, please send immediately!

BING

A bottle of professional-grade acetone tipped over, and its contents spilled across the white tile of the nail spa floor, sneaking into the valleys of the mildewed grout and running toward my *tsinelas*. When the liquid quickly bore a hole through the sole of my sandals, I understood why Ma's hands rotted away despite her wearing latex gloves.

Ma fingered the mask off her face and gestured with her lips toward a mop for me to clean up the mess, so I put down my homework and did what I was told. I didn't mind, since Mrs Finnegan assigns the most mundane homework—reading flimsy seventy-five-page books, doing book reports mostly with drawings, observing the effects of placing cardboard on patches of grass—that is not, in my opinion, suitable for grade three. It is practically daycare. I would rather listen to the Vietnamese ladies chime amongst themselves while complaining about the very women whose feet they are tending to.

"They're just like us Filipinos," said Ma one day, when I stayed with her until closing. "But their fish sauce is sweeter, and they have no Spanish in their language." This is why I do not understand the Vietnamese ladies' conversation. I think of it more like music from a radio that I can tune this way and that. Like our words in Filipino, only cut short in snippets of white paper dolls, masked ladies squatting side by side, one, then the other, then the other.

While I pushed the mop across the floor, I watched a snowstorm of callous descend onto Ma's pedicure towel. Ma held the white lady's foot inches from her eyes, peeling the woman like a damaged carrot. The white lady was overwhelmed by her ticklishness, which made Ma hold the foot firmer, like a lamb ready for shearing. Ma filed the white lady's toenails into perfect rounded squares and buffed the surface. She began to prod the white lady with her metal pusher, abusing the cuticle into submission with every scrape, shovelling out ancient filth, slicing the cuticle off the moon-shaped eponychium at the top of the nail, all while the white lady screamed and pleaded. Even massage was torture for the white lady, so Ma resorted to simply pounding her fists into the white lady's soles. Patience was running thin. Finally, Ma painted. Base coat. Two coats of colour. Topcoat.

Just as the white lady began to talk about how much she hated her mother-in-law, Ma said, "Enjoy!" and expertly ushered the white lady to a nail drying chair. Ma switched the fan to maximum to drown out the end of the white lady's obnoxious story.

"You can't massage white people's feet for too long," Ma once told me while massaging the growing pains out of my legs. "*Yang mga puti.* Those white people. That's the way they are. They have a bad energy. They think their lives have so many problems when they don't. And when you massage their feet, all their sadness goes into your body."

Ma gestured toward my homework. "Okay, Bing. Show me."

I reluctantly opened my pink-lined notebook. She asked for the assignment paper from Mrs Finnegan.

"*Ano ito?*" She flipped the page toward me with a confused look on her face.

"We have to draw a picture of what I want to be when I grow up."

Her face twisted at the picture I had drawn: me looking up into the heavens, a choir of angels singing my praises.

"*Anak*, you want to be Jesus?"

"No, Ma. I want to be a saint."

"That is not a job." She removed her latex gloves by turning them inside out, then tossed them into the garbage bin. The fingers of the gloves were already eaten away by one service. Talcum powder outlined her nails and rashes.

"Why?"

"Well ... it's not a job until you're dead."

I tried to convince her as we closed the shop and began walking our usual path behind the nail salon to our high-rise apartment. "Isn't it a job to do saintly things while you're alive?"

"No one pays for saintliness, *anak*."

That night, as I pretended to sleep, I heard the sound of my mother's ivory bracelets clanking against each other as she slowly made her way to my bedroom. I felt the light from the hallway paint my eyelids warm, and I tried not to quicken my breath.

This is her nightly ritual. She kneels at the side of my bed, her body grunting from a day's work, her knees clicking, her wrists twisting to support her weight upon descent. Her calloused hands brush through my hair. It feels so good. Better than the night before. Not as good as tomorrow.

She made the sign of the cross on my forehead, the ivory cool against my skin. "Dear God," she began. "Please let Bing live a long, happy, healthy life." That covered all the bases: her son safe, pleased with himself, and with no tragic end, for there was already enough tragedy for a lifetime.

She quietly left, as she always does, and when the door slid shut, the room was so cold. My skin was hungry, my heart felt full, wishing she would stroke my hair all night long.

Once I awoke to my mother screaming. She was screaming and doing. Always a multitasker, my mother. Dishes and phone calls. Laundry and opening mail. But this time, she was screaming while packing. She was stuffing a fabric-covered granny cart with underwear and clothes for me and for her. It was like one task could not be complete without the other. She was a soldier screaming a battle cry before doing the deed of murder. She was escaping despite every muscle in her body begging her to stay and continue being hurt.

"Ma?" I wiped away the crusts from the corners of my eyes. Was I dreaming? I opened up my mouth to speak again. My voice was hoarse. "Ma? What's happening? What's wrong?"

"Weeee ... weeeee ... neeed ... to ... to ..." I couldn't understand what she was saying. Waves of sorrow ripped through her. Every sound was a struggle. She was getting so lost in her vowels that she'd misplace the end of the word. I was worried she was going to vomit. But she kept hustling back and forth from the granny cart to my chest of drawers. Between her sobs was the slap slap of her *tsinelas* against the bottom of her feet. My face must have caught her attention because she paused long enough to kneel before my bed, hold my hand in hers, and look me right in the eye.

"Listen, *anak*. Liss ... listen." She wiped her nose on her sleeve. "We have to leave here. It's no longer safe." She buried her head in my lap and wept. I stroked her hair gently. It was wet, either with tears or sweat, I wasn't sure.

I began nodding my head while I scrunched my face up, crying. I knew what we were doing. We were leaving Daddy. I got up, an obedient son, and began dressing in my day clothes, but Ma stopped me.

"We dooon't have tiiime. Just put your jaacket ... jack ... jacket on."

There was a firm knock on the door. We both jumped at the sound. Those kinds of sounds had happened all the time with Daddy. Ma looked cautiously through the peephole, then opened it.

"Hey, Bernard." Tita Mae entered with a sad face, seeing I had already been told the news. Tita Mae, who was Ma's first friend when we arrived in Canada, had a car and was going to drive us all the way from Moss Park to Scarborough to keep us safe. Tita Mae looked at Ma, and they held each other, both of them sniffling into each other's shoulders. Unlike Ma's dishevelled state, Tita Mae's hair was blow-dried straight, and her blue patterned leggings ended with the dazzle of silver on her mule shoes. In contrast to Tita Mae, I could sense how undone Ma was, how she had been for a while since Daddy started changing.

"Is this all you're bringing?" Tita Mae pointed to the granny cart. Ma nodded. "Are you sure?"

"We have to hurry. I don't have time to pack more. He might be home soon." Ma looked at the door expectantly.

"Edna. What will he do if he comes home?! He'll have to get past me first." Tita Mae's Vietnamese clip of her consonants contrasted heavily with Ma's wailing vowels. Ma wearily went to the washroom and packed our toothbrushes.

Tita Mae looked around and found my jacket. She gently placed it on my shoulders. "Get your arms in, Bernard." She knew she was waking me from a nightmare. She had done this before: helping people escape, or escaping herself. I felt numb and did as I was told. She kissed me on the forehead and hugged me tight. "Let's go."

I sat in my pyjamas in the back of Tita Mae's car with Ma. I held her hand. As we merged onto the Don Valley Parkway, Ma wailed helplessly. I continued to look out the window. I remember watching each exit on the 401 pass us, one more vein of connection severed from a man we no longer recognized.

"Edna? Bernard? Do you want breakfast?" Tita Mae held up a bag with two wrapped *bánh mì*. She passed it back to me. I reached for it and held it like a baby. Ma and I could not eat. I was too busy holding Ma's hand.

Tita Mae looked at Ma through the rear-view mirror. "Edna, you can start working at the nail salon with me. I'll teach you. No problem. You can stay with me until you find a place." She shifted her gaze to me. I could only see her eyes, but I knew she was trying to smile at me. She was trying to tell me that we were going to be okay. She just didn't know how, so she smiled instead.

I knew then this was not the time to tell Ma that my daddy had put my hand under the hot water tap until it burned, or that he had ordered me to hide in my room because I was so fat and ugly. I would tell her later, when she doubted her choice to leave someone so ill in his mind and heart.

CORY

Cory received the call at the RV plant on an unusually cold night in September.

Penetrating through the noise of spinning screws and the wafts of formaldehyde, his boss's voice called him away from the assembly line to answer the phone. It was Jessica.

He took the orange industrial-strength earplug out of his right ear and put the receiver to it. "I left her in the bowling alley," she explained. Past tense. Cory dropped the phone and ran toward the parking lot. He ran as fast as he could to the car and brushed just enough frost off the windshield to peek through it at the road ahead. It would take him a solid eight minutes to get to Island Road from Coronation Drive.

When he arrived, he made a beeline toward the Pins and Needles bowling alley, his tire marks diagonal across the slush-covered parking lot. The wooden doors were so heavy, Cory couldn't get them open fast enough. He was greeted by an elderly Asian woman spraying bowling shoes with one hand and adjusting her dollar store glasses with the other.

"She's over there," said the lady disapprovingly. "Your wife just left her here all alone. You can't do that here!"

Laura sat there, waiting as still as a statue, with two plastic bags, one on her lap, the other holding up her elbow like the armrest on a chair. She sat there, her tiny red fists disciplined around the handles, and stared into space. Thinking what? Cory wondered. He scooped

Laura up and felt the sinew of her, the sheer lightness of her body, and then he held her close and tight.

"Oh, God. Oh, no. Oh, nooooo. It's Daddy. It's Daddy. I'm here now."

"Did you hear me?" The bowling alley lady interrupted their reunion. "You tell your wife—"

"She's not my wife." Cory didn't want to look the lady in the eye. *Fucking chink.*

The lady quickly and efficiently repositioned a line of bowling shoes so she could lift the flap of the counter. She emerged on the other side to confront Cory, her chest puffed like a peacock, proud and ready for battle.

"You don't leave children alone like that. She's just a baby."

"Get out of my face." *This greasy bitch is really asking for it.*

"I asked her if she wanted chips, and she said no. She is so skinny. Take her home and feed her. Now get out."

The lady opened the door of the bowling alley. The cold snap was in full swing. Winter blew through the lady's bangs like a warning.

Cory swung his prize daughter into the passenger seat of his car. Now was his chance to warm it up. Get it nice and toasty; point all the vents toward his princess, and blast hot air at her. As the windows defrosted, Cory ran his rough hands, his dirt-stained hands, through her frozen strawberry blond hair and sobbed openly. Through his wailing, he blubbered, "We're gonna pass by Timmy Ho's and get you a hot chocolate. Warm you right up. Daddy loves you. Were you in there for long, Laura? I'm really sorry. I would have come sooner, but Mommy just called me." He wasn't sure how much she understood, but her gaze was steady on his weepy eyes.

It must have been either the monotonous swish of the wipers or the hiss of the heater vents, but Laura was fast asleep within minutes of finding shelter in her father's beat-up Toyota Corolla. Her head shifted to the side, and the fabric of the seat belt pressed into the chub of her right cheek as she dreamt of blowing dandelions and making wishes spread across grassy fields. Cory watched her pink lips surrender to slumber. He needed to get a kid's seat, he realized; better leave it for the next day. For now, sleep ... and dodging the cops, in case they see his six-year-old sitting shotgun without a proper booster seat.

He pulled into the parking lot of his apartment at Morningside and Lawrence Avenues. He undid her seat belt and unleashed her limp skinny frame on to his body. *Finally. My girl.* The delicious point of her chin biting into his trapezius, her hands swaying with each step he took. Cory's boots rubbed against the stained sisal carpeting. Through the lobby, where he saw Mrs Khan carting in her groceries. Down the hallway, to the tune of the humming fluorescent tube lighting. He wondered suddenly—the elevator, where there may be arguments about the laundry room, or the stairs, where the slamming of doors echoed in the stairwell. Elevator, Cory decided. He got on the elevator with that Filipina lady who works at the nail salon and her fat son. She always held him close and averted eye contact when Cory rode up with them. Tonight was no different, despite his having a sleeping girl over his shoulder. Suited Cory just fine. He winced at the smell of fried garlic on their jackets. The doors opened at his floor to a combination of canned laughter and heavy-handed soundtracks blasting through the thin walls, the sound of televisions being watched in each household like an escape, like a babysitter in a box. Suite 367, talk show baby-daddy drama. Suite 368, renovation reality show. Suite 369, children's cartoon. Finally, suite 370. As quietly as possible, Cory pulled out his keys, pushed them into the lock, and opened the door.

He lay his daughter on the bed face up, which made her snore so perfectly. She was the most beautiful sack of potatoes he ever did see. He removed her wet sneakers and silently placed them on the baseboard heater, despite it working only intermittently. It would have to do for now, he thought. Her pants were soaked, pee or snow, he couldn't tell. He removed those as well, Laura's legs like dead weights falling on to the bed with each pant leg being pulled off. Cory drew the covers all the way up to her chin and, even in her sleep, could see Laura's relief at the sensation of dry warmth.

When morning broke, it was Wednesday. Cory was able to ask his manager for another nighttime shift, so he could get Laura registered for school.

I can do this. I can do this. Cory placed his last waffle from the freezer into the toaster, then rifled through his daughter's plastic bags for a change of clothes. *I can do this. I can do this.* The toaster popped a steaming waffle from its grate. He promptly picked it up and dropped it on the counter. *Motherfucker! Ow! That's hot! I can do this. I can do this.* He found another set of purple undies and had Laura step into them. He realized he had slipped the undies over her pants instead of underneath them. *Fucking hell. I can do this. I can do this.* He took off Laura's pants, put her undies on, grabbed the now cool waffle, and placed it in her mouth like a dog's chew toy. *No time to brush her teeth. Don't have a toothbrush anyway. Gotta buy that. Toothbrush. I can do this. I can do this.* He zipped up her jacket, got her shoes on. *Shit. She needs a bag. One of those backpacks. Toothbrush. Backpack. Got it.* He took one of her grocery bags and filled it with a spare set of clothes, in case she had an accident, and a ballpoint pen. He handed the bag to Laura for her to carry.

"You ready, kiddo?" Laura nodded.

The frosty weather from the night before had dissipated into a crisp autumn morning. They speed-walked south from their apartment building on Morningside toward the school. Cory noticed Laura looking over her shoulder. When he looked behind them, he saw that Filipina nail lady and her fat son also making their way from the apartment to the school. The fat kid waved at Laura.

"Hurry up, Laura Loo. We gotta hustle and sign you up." Cory used his arm to encourage Laura's gaze forward.

As soon as the doors to Rouge Hill Public School opened, Cory rushed Laura down the hall to the school office.

A tall Black woman sat behind the desk with a nameplate saying, "Mrs Crosby, Secretary."

Cory took off his snap-back Argos cap and brushed his fingers through his overgrown, greasy blond hair. He hoisted Laura up and sat her beside the desk on a wooden bench reserved for detentions.

"I'll need you fill out some things," said Mrs Crosby, awkwardly making her way to a steel filing cabinet with her pleather mule shoes slapping the soles of her feet. Cory rolled his eyes at Mrs Crosby's choice of loud-patterned dress and uncomfortable footwear. *Typical of them,* he thought. *Always wanting to be seen.*

Once back behind her desk, she placed an inch-thick pile of paperwork on the counter. "Do you have her ID?"

Cory's jaw tightened. *She thinks she's so high and mighty just because she's sitting behind a desk.*

"Jesus. I think I left it at the house," Cory replied, not wanting to get into the details about his crazy bitch of an ex, how that welfare queen almost cost him his job, how he is pretty sure Jessica never fed Laura let alone got her a birth certificate, how he's not sure how often a kid should be taken to the washroom, how he forgot to prepare Laura's lunch, how Jessica made him the happiest man in the world twice in his lifetime: once, giving birth to Laura, and once, leaving Laura behind.

"Can I get back to you?" *Toothbrush. Backpack. ID.*

Mrs Crosby's eyes knowingly darted between Cory and Laura. At a school in an at-risk neighbourhood, their "Don't Ask, Don't Tell" policy was used often, usually with undocumented folks.

"Do you have any proof of residence?"

What does she think? That I'm some kind of criminal? I just want to bring my kid to school. "I have my driver's licence."

She looked at his name.

"Okay, Mr Mitkowski. You are in our catchment area, so she can attend Rouge Hill, and she will most likely start next week. We have to figure out which grade one classroom she will be in. When you can, can you please bring me her health card?"

He nodded, completely unsure.

"Does she have any allergies or any other health risks we should know about? Has she had her immunizations?"

He shook his head, completely unsure.

"When we have figured out which classroom she will attend, I will give you a call. Most likely, due to numbers, she will be in Mrs Landau's class, but we want to confirm this first. Can you give me a phone number where you can be reached during the day?"

Cory nodded and recited the number.

Mrs Crosby tilted her body to the side to smile tightly at Cory. "For now, until you hear back from us, we have the Ontario Reads Literacy Centre just down the hallway here." She looked at the weathered Food Basics plastic bag atop Laura's lap, her fists tight around the bag's handle.

"And they serve food there, if you want to join them." Another tight smile.

Those were the magic words. All the poor kids knew how to follow the smell of Cheerios to their next free meal. Cory, awakened by his purebred white trash instincts cultivated by years of food bank smarts, followed the stream of stained, ill-fitting jogging pant-wearing children to a schoolroom that seemed to host a breakfast program. You could tell these kids needed it most. There were no back-to-school fashion ensembles here. Goodwill Keds, used year round, were as close as they would get to winter boots, as close as they would get to sandals. The ends of sleeves tucked into frostbitten fists were as close as they would get to mittens, and were rolled up in summer months to fend off the heat.

Standing near the frame of a doorless cupboard filled with the coveted Cheerios was a dark brown woman. She adjusted her hijab as she took inventory of the shelved food. She caught eyes with Laura and smiled.

Fuck. A towelhead, Cory thought.

"Good morning," she said. "Come on in. My name is Ms Hina. Did you want to come in to play?"

Cory could see that despite her smile, Ms Hina was eyeing Laura`s randomly and unevenly shorn hair. Cory had the same haircut in school after a bout of lice. It always looks like badly mowed grass. Like an emergency.

Laura stood silently by the door, her face red with embarrassment.

"We were just having some breakfast. Did you want to eat?"

Laura`s hunger pulled her away from the doorframe. Cory allowed her to enter this classroom-cum-breakfast-room-cum-daycare with a protective arm around her, trying to keep his daughter away from the smell of curry, likely from that Paki teacher. Laura squeaked as she walked toward the cupboard, her sneakers still wet from the night before.

While Cory stood cautiously over her, Laura ate Cheerios until Ms Hina had no more milk in the fridge to accompany it. Laura then resorted to eating the cereal dry by the fistful. When she had her fill of food, she sat on the centre`s rocking chair, rocking back and forth and silently watching an inexplicable circle of light dance around the room.

"You see that?" asked Ms Hina, pointing at the flash of light. "I think that's from my wristwatch."

Laura observed Ms Hina twisting her wrist to catch the sunlight, like it was magic on the ceiling, magic on Laura's palms, magic on her cheeks.

Cory's face was red, what with this towelhead observing the state of their trashiness, acute poverty hanging like the mucus drying under Laura's nose. He cautiously removed his black satin bomber jacket, glancing at the stitched-on logo of a Prussian eagle from back in his days of shaved heads and beers with the boys, and sat down on one of the school chairs. His knees were too high for comfort, despite being short for an adult. He used his jacket to cover the Iron Cross tattoo on his forearm.

"I'm going to give you this," Ms Hina said to Cory before they were set to leave. It was an information pamphlet on lice removal. "I know that lice shampoo is expensive, so I have this large bottle of olive oil. We use it here at the centre for making playdough. But we have more than enough. You can take it home with you. Just apply it to her head for the next three days, and let her sleep with it on. Remove the nits, and clean her clothes. Works just as well, if not better, than lice shampoo. But we will need her to be treated before she can return to the centre."

Cory snatched the pamphlet and the olive oil from that Paki, powerless to this brown woman he hated so, for he, too, was hungry for Cheerios.

After school, back at the apartment, poor Laura looked like she had been licked by a dog, there was so much oil everywhere. Cory did all the laundry by hand in the bathtub, using Palmolive dish soap from the food bank. His little girl was oily, shiny, sticky, and without lice. Anything to get free breakfast in the morning.

DAILY REPORT

September 22, 2011

Facilitator: Hina Hassani

Location: Rouge Hill Public School

Attendance:

Parent/Guardian/Caregiver	Children (one per line please)
Cory Mitkowski	Laura Mitkowski
Edna Espiritu	Bernard Espiritu
Helen McKay	Finnegan Everson
	Liam Williams
	Sebastian Dennis
	Chloe Smith
Fern Donahue	Paulo Sanchez
	Kyle Keegan
Marie Beaudoin	Sylvie Beaudoin
	Johnny Beaudoin
Pamela Roy	Evan Roy
	Yanna Roy
	Tasha Roy
Lily Chan	Aiden Chan
	Jennifer Chan
Amina Mohammed	Waleed Mohammed

Notes:

Much better attendance today. My biggest grab seems to be parents who have kids on their way to school. That thirty minutes before the national anthem is when this place is packed with children. They play, eat breakfast, then head to their classrooms. Those moms or dads who want a place to play with their younger preschool kids will stick around. I am thrilled word is spreading.

Today's favourite activities included the water table, much to the chagrin of the grownups. I've had numerous complaints about it, as we're heading into fall and winter. Purple-dyed water was drunk by the handful or splashed on other children. It was a bit disastrous. Parents and caregivers are asking if we can nix the water table and perhaps replace it with shredded paper or other found objects. They just don't want the kids to be catching colds or other nasty bugs. Let me know your thoughts. It may have been a full moon, but circle time was also equally disastrous. I almost lost my voice trying to sing songs with the kids, they were so rowdy. They all just wanted to keep playing with the water table. Ha!

There are two older kids who seem to enjoy each other's company, Bing and Sylvie. Today I gave them both the task of creating their own comic books. Sylvie agreed to write the story, and Bing agreed to illustrate it. Bing's teacher, Mrs Finnegan, has asked me for my thoughts on whether or not Bing should be assessed for giftedness designation. I agree that he should, but I will get back to her next week with my formal thoughts.

There is a father, Cory, who comes in here with his daughter Laura. I am not sure what their story is yet, but Laura often comes in pretty hungry. I would ask what the situation is, but the dad seems rather antisocial toward me. I am going to strategize over the next couple weeks about some ways to gently integrate Laura in with the other children.

Weekly supplies requested:

2% milk	three bags, please
crackers	one box
cream cheese	two tubs
Shreddies	two boxes
raisins	one box, bulk
carrots	shredded carrots, please! The toddlers seem to find it easier to eat. Maybe the other centres would benefit, too—less coughing up orange all over the tables. ☺

oatmeal	one large bag, quick oats
yogurt	small serving sizes, variety of flavours

Jane Fulton <jfulton@ontarioreads.ca>
September 22, 2011
11:50 a.m. (8 hours ago)
To <hhassani@ontarioreads.ca>

Hi, Hina.

Thanks so much for your detailed notes. We are so happy that attendance is increasing at the new Rouge Hill Public School centre. These numbers are crucial since our funding depends on solid statistics. Having these forms truly helps our marketing and development officer get those dollars put toward each centre!

May I suggest you take some time to flyer the neighbourhood around the centre as part of the outreach to get those numbers even higher? This strategy has worked well in our downtown Toronto locations, and given the vastness of the geography of the suburbs, I imagine this kind of outreach would be even more effective in Scarborough.

I want to give you a word of caution about making food the main draw for families. We know you are located in a low-income neighbourhood, and I want to assure you that the resources are there to feed these community members elsewhere. That's why we provide small portions of snacks, but the serving of a formal breakfast sends the wrong message. The focus of the centres is to encourage healthy parenting and literacy. So while food is included in our programming, the purpose is school readiness, since sharing food will be a part of the daily life of a student. The centre is not, however, a soup kitchen.

If you need clarification, please let me know.

Take care and great work!

Jane Fulton, MSW

Supervisor, Ontario Reads Program

Reading is a way for me to expand my mind, open my eyes, and fill up my heart.

—Oprah Winfrey

Me <hhassani@ontarioreads.ca>
September 22, 2011
1:15 a.m. (6 hours ago)
To Jane Fulton <jfulton@ontarioreads.ca>

Hello, Jane:

Thanks for your feedback. Are other facilitators across the province doing the same flyering you are suggesting? Also, I am wondering if this time doing "outreach" will be included in my paid work schedule or if this will be paid outside of my schedule on an hourly basis? Please advise. I know community-building is part of my job description, but off-site activity was not part of my contract.

Re: serving food at the centre. If there were thirty attendees throughout the day

who also happened to be present for snack
time, would it look any different than thirty children who are fed in the morning
before school, using the same supplies we
would use for snacks? And know that this
is far from a "formal breakfast." I'm just
substituting cheese and crackers with more
oatmeal and yogurts, for example. I'm not
trying to be adversarial; however, I do
feel the centre is being used appropriate-
ly, since servings of breakfast seem to be
needed in this neighbourhood.

I would love to discuss this with you
further. Are you available to drop by
during our centre hours sometime next week?
Sincerely,
Hina Hassani, Facilitator
Ontario Reads Program, Rouge Hill Public
School

Jane Fulton <jfulton@ontarioreads.ca>
September 22, 2011
2:30 p.m. (5 hours ago)
To <hhassani@ontarioreads.ca>

Hi, Hina.
We can most definitely discuss this. But
since our main office is located downtown,
perhaps we can do so at your next performance review, in November. (In the meantime, I would love your thoughts on where
you can flyer. There are so many opportuni-

ties for connection that I don't want you
to miss. ☺)

I assure you that the centres were de-
signed after years of trial and error.
We pride ourselves on solid relation-
ship-building with communities, and I tell
you now that dangling food in front of hungry people is not what draws parents back
to your site. They love having a warm cup
of coffee in the morning while their kids
enjoy circle time. They love watching their
children run around during gym. We are
trying to cultivate the next generation of
good parents, not just full tummies. I know
your sentiments, and I have felt them too.
Trust me.

As for flyering, I am sure it won't take
too much time between your leaving work and
dropping them off at a few apartment build-
ings. That Native Child and Family Services
place is also right around the corner,
don't forget!

Again, great work. I am so pleased to
have a worker with their wheels turning!
Cheers!
Jane Fulton, MSW
Supervisor, Ontario Reads Program
*Reading is a way for me to expand my mind,
open my eyes, and fill up my heart.*
        —Oprah Winfrey

LAURA

"Why is your hair so oily?" asked the fancy girl during lunch recess while she twirled the plastic handle of a skipping rope. The girl wore a plum red beret positioned neatly to one side. She rubbed her perfect button nose while she surveyed Laura's getup: My Little Pony lunch bag, blue leggings, quilted red jacket, oily hair.

"Ah, come on, Clara. Why aren't you turning the rope?" said a brown girl behind her.

"Are you new?" Clara kept her eyes on Laura, who nodded silently. Clara looked at the brown girl and screamed, "I think she's new!"

The brown girl approached with the other end of the skipping rope. Although she was only a few inches taller than Laura, she crouched down and placed her hands on her knees, like she was looking at an injured animal. "What's your name, sweetie?" She sounded like a grown-up.

"Laura." She looked down at her shoes.

"My name is Sylvie."

"You're dirty," said Clara.

"Goddamn it, Clara. That's why my mama says you're nothing but a snooty bitch." Sylvie snatched the other end of the skipping rope from Clara's hands and skipped away, the rope all to herself.

"That's it! I'm telling Mrs Finnegan!"

"Go on. If you tell, I'll never let you play with my skipping rope."

"I've got five skipping ropes at home. I don't care!"

"I don't care either. I know your dad doesn't let you bring your skipping ropes to school cuz he thinks everyone's gonna steal them from you, because you're a rich, snooty bitch."

They continued their bickering while Laura quietly made her way to the side entrance. She watched as a flurry of children exited, then she sneaked in while the door was open. The school felt so different without children inside it. It felt kind of nice. Laura looked around at all the drawings on the walls, at all the indoor shoes lined up outside each closed classroom door.

One door remained open. Classical music was playing on a radio. With yellow rubber gloves on, Ms Hina walked to the radio and turned the volume up before continuing her wipe-down of a box of wooden blocks. Three toddlers quietly played around a sandbox in the middle of the room while their parents chatted over coffee. Ms Hina saw Laura in the frame of the door and removed her gloves.

"Hi, Laura." She knelt down to meet her eyes. "It was nice seeing you yesterday. How are you today?"

Laura shrugged.

"Are you supposed to be outside playing?"

Laura shrugged.

Ms Hina spied Laura's My Little Pony lunch bag and her tiny fingers wrapped tightly around the handle. "That's a cool bag! Can I see?" Laura showed her, half smiling. "I love My Little Pony. My favourite one is Minty because I love green and pink." Laura grinned widely. Minty was her favourite, too. Carefully, and with a warm smile, Ms Hina asked, "Can I see inside your lunch bag?" Laura's face flushed. She nodded yes. The lunch bag was empty. Ms Hina took a breath. "What a beautiful lunch bag. I bet cold things stay cold, and hot things stay hot in here." Ms Hina stood up and looked around the room. "Guess what today was? It was make your own muffin day. While the school-agers were in class, all the parents learned how to make yummy oatmeal muffins. Do you want one?" Laura nodded. Ms Hina grabbed one of the muffins and an apple from the fridge, then placed them inside Laura's lunch bag. "There you go."

"Daddy says you eat babies."

Ms Hina paused, then smiled. "Do you think I eat babies?"

Laura shook her head.

"No. I don't eat babies, that's for sure. I love eating carrot cake and coffee. What do you like to eat?"

Laura shrugged her shoulders. "What's that?" Laura pointed to Ms Hina's hijab.

"It's my hijab."

"Why do you wear that?"

Ms Hina paused, "Because it reminds me of who I am."

They stood for a brief moment looking at each other. Ms Hina took another breath, then headed to a storage cabinet. She returned with a small foam letter *h* and held it inches away from Laura's face. Magic.

"Do you know what letter this is?" Laura shrugged. "It's the letter *h*. Every letter makes a sound. And all those sounds together make a word. And all those words together can make a story." Ms Hina placed her hand in front of her face and exhaled to make a huh sound. "Huh–huh–horse. If I give you this letter, can you promise to give it back to me?" Laura reached out for the letter. "But," Ms Hina pulled it away playfully, "you have to tell me words that make a huh sound. You pinky promise?" Ms Hina presented her pinky finger. Laura linked her finger. A deal.

"Okay. You'd better go outside and play. And let me know if those oatmeal muffins are any good, okay?"

Laura scurried out to recess, lunch bag and all.

BING

"It seems Bernard here had a bit of an incident on the bus today," Principal Sankiewicz reported solemnly to Edna, summarizing the incident succinctly. "A couple of the grade sixers were a bit rough with him. We had some words with them, and we think it's in Bernard's best interest to head home for some rest."

The clock on the wall behind Ma's confused face ticked relentlessly. Sankiewicz compared the time with the clock on his iPhone. Two minutes faster.

The principal's condensed and abridged description of the afternoon's bus ride from the Toronto Zoo left out numerous details. He failed to tell Ma that I had been struggling to open the wrapper of my granola bar when the back of my head was swiftly slapped by Aiden Redden, who's in grade six.

"Stop eating, you fat fuck," Aiden said, his look of disgust framed by his Justin Bieber mop.

For a reason I still cannot understand myself, I got onto my knees to search the ridged floor of the bus for the remains of my granola bar.

Cole Hester, also in grade six, seized the opportunity to step on my hand with his second-hand Blundstone boots. I yelped, and the children squealed with laughter.

Mrs Emerson, who reluctantly sat at the front of the bus, ordered everyone to quiet down. They did. But the torture continued, just quietly.

Aiden rallied everyone to loom over me on the floor of the bus, helpless and crying.

"Open up your lunches. This beached whale needs to be fed."

Bologna. Crackers. Cheese strings. Cellophane. It all hit my face with such hatred.

"Sto-o-op! Stop it now!" said a voice that no one listened to. I felt a sweaty hand grasp the fabric of my button-up shirt and pull me up. It was Sylvie. She looked down at my pants, and I was ashamed at what she saw. She opened the window, told me to sit, took off her sweater, and handed it to me. "Go on, put it around your waist to hide everything," she said. She crossed her arms and looked out at the distance to ensure I didn't feel embarrassed. The hair standing up on her arms told me she needed her sweater back, but I had no choice.

After we left the principal's office, I whispered the obvious into Ma's ear. "I pooped my pants." The teachers refused to clean me up.

Ma choked on her tears.

The rest of that entire day, I sat on her lap, clean, with hair still wet from a long bubble bath. We watched anything and everything on TV, while she caressed my skin with her motherly touches. I am loved. I will be loved. I am loved. I will be loved. I am perfect just the way I am. She has me repeat it. I practically suffocated under her loving grasp, but I dared not escape.

For the rest of my life, I will remember the names of Cole Hester and Aiden Redden. Their faces and names are etched on my chest. I will remember the bus driver who saw it all through the rear-view mirror, his eyes looking listlessly at me as I cried for help. I will remember Mrs Emerson and her empty orders. I will remember Principal Sankiewicz and his abridged version of what happened to me. I will remember Sylvie and her sweater around my waist, hiding my poop-stained pants.

But at that moment, on my mother's lap, I languished in the sheer size of me. I was forced to rejoice in every fingernail, every hair on my head, the dimples in my cheeks. She kissed my eyelids so fiercely, in a Filipino way, her lips pressed together to reveal no lip. More a smell than a smooch.

SYLVIE

Mama had another emergency. Something about Daddy's medication for his pain. Again we were at Mr George's door, and I was looking forward to more throat hole gazing and *Wheel of Fortune*. But the old man was not there. No matter how many times Mama knocked, it didn't change the answer. She had to find another way to leave me with someone so that she, Johnny, and Daddy could make it to Scarborough General Hospital during clinic hours.

Mama gave up and decided to take me along. With Daddy hobbling along on his crutches, our plan was to ride the bus to Lawrence Avenue, then head west toward the hospital. But as we were transferring, I tugged at Mama's arm. I could see my friend Bing through the window of Incredible Nails Salon, which is sandwiched between Tarek's Convenience and Halal, and the Oasis Spa. I removed the hood of my red coat so he could recognize me. We waved at each other, both of us making fog circles on our sides of the window.

"Not now, Sylvie!" and Mama tugged back. I shook her hand off and ran inside the salon, much to Mama's dismay. "The 54 bus is coming. We have to leave!" She struggled with the salon door and the stroller. Daddy waited outside, leaning on his crutches.

"You want pedicure?" asked one of the Vietnamese ladies at the counter, the dangling gold bell still ringing as I ran in and hugged Bing. Mama gave her that look she often gave to Asians. *Can't I walk in here without you pestering me to pay for something?* The Vietnamese lady gave Mama a look that we often got for being Indigenous. *In or out? Pay or go? Make up your mind, you nasty Native.*

"Marie?" Bing's mom, Edna, left her pedicure station with a look of concern behind her medical mask. Edna went behind the reception desk and grabbed my sweater, now clean, and handed it to Mama, then they both looked at me and smiled. Mama and Edna exchanged a few words, and the next thing I knew, I was staying the entire day with Bing. I wasn't sure how it was possible, as Bing was supposed to be at school, too. Something about him being sad that day, after what I saw on the bus. Edna was happy he had a playmate. Mama was happy she could ride the bus in some peace while Johnny napped and Daddy groaned in pain.

After Bing and I got bored playing checkers with the nail polish bottles, he suggested we venture outside the nail salon.

"We have to wait until one of the white ladies comes in. Then Ma won't notice."

We watched a client enter the salon. Edna pulled her eyes away from the news broadcast on the television that hung on the wall and gestured to the white lady to sit at the pedicure station. Once she turned on the spa jets, Bing and I were out the back door, zipping up our coats.

"Where are we going?" I asked Bing as we crept out like two spies. From the back of the nail salon I could see the towering verandas of an apartment complex that looked down on the back of the strip mall.

"To see Ivana."

Ivana had an air to her, like she knew everyone either hated her or wanted her, or both. She stood outside the back of Oasis Spa, smoking a cigarette. Despite the autumn breeze, her stringy blonde hair clung to her forehead and steam glowed from the skin that was exposed beyond her bomber jacket.

"Bing!" she called out. She flashed a pink lipstick smile. We ran toward her. She reached into her pocket and handed Bing a pair of sunglasses. Bing marvelled at Ivana's newest acquisition, placing them on his round face, the non-existent bridge of his nose barely holding the sunglasses on his chubby cheeks.

"They don't want people to know they come here for tugs, so they wear these," Ivana explained, adjusting the glasses on Bing's smiling cheeks. "And if I'm lucky, they sometimes forget them." By the way she said it, raising her eyebrows, I knew it had something to do with sex. She looked at me, gauging my reaction to her profession. She decided to continue.

"I also found this." Taking out a lighter with a woman on it, Ivana demonstrated how to reveal the woman's breasts by lighting the lighter. Although the look of it gave me a sick feeling in my vagina, I was perplexed at how the illusion was achieved. She showed me over and over again, until her phone vibrated in her pocket. She looked at the text message, then at me.

"Here, you have it." She placed the found object in my hand before heading back to work. A jewel.

After Mama picked me up, I rushed into our suite, and I placed the naked lady lighter in my Forever Box under my bed. Mama gave me the box after my birthday.

It wasn't a birthday present, but something to make up for the birthday present Johnny ruined. My real present was a super difficult fifty-piece puzzle. It was a picture of a seagull flying through the air.

What made it difficult were the hundreds of shades of white, blue, and grey that made up the clouds. It wasn't as difficult as keeping it away from Johnny, though. I tried to start it on the floor, but of course Johnny wouldn't have it. He loves to dismantle things. Like shoelaces tied up, or the cupboards closed, or zippers zipped up. They make him furious. This puzzle was no different.

The truth is, I know Mama gave me this puzzle to keep me busy for as long as possible, because Johnny is worth the trouble of three screaming kids. So I learned pretty early to play by myself for long periods of time. Until time was lost. Until the sun went down, and suddenly Mama would tell me it's time for bed. She would pat me on the head, thankful for my independence. "You had a good day, missy?" she would say just before laying out my pyjamas. I always nodded.

Unlike my Ballerina Barbie, unlike my ZhuZhu Pet, which Johnny ignored, he had to tear apart my puzzle like he needed to itch a scratch. There was no floor space; there was no corner; there was no table safe from his swiping arm, back and forth across the puzzle pieces.

"Puzzles aren't permanent, eh?" Mama told me. I knew that. I just wanted to be able to finish it. Just once. "It means you get to have fun building it over and over again."

My face went hot. I wanted to hit her. I wanted to hit my brother. I dug my fingernails into my palms instead, making white-knuckle fists.

I agreed to let Johnny have three pieces, to put together and take apart as much as he liked, so as to leave me alone with the remainder of the image. And when I agreed, I mean I nodded the smallest nod you can ever imagine, my teeth gnashing and my lips tight. Only uncaring, insensitive, neglectful mothers would have read that nod as a yes. And guess what? She did. Johnny was placed on my bed with his three pieces. Mama took a breath and tried to wash out underwear in the bathroom sink. I went back to work on the floor, trying to connect the point of the seagull's beak to the eyes on its head. That's when I heard Johnny choking.

"Goddamn it! Johnny!" Mama rushed over and hooked her finger inside his mouth to fish out soggy pieces of cardboard that were blocking his breathing. He vomited what looked like the seagull's webbed feet. All over my bed. She looked at me with a half-smile, half-sorry face.

I screamed and threw the puzzle pieces in random directions around the room. I whipped my arms frantically, hoping Mama's or Johnny's face might find their way into my fists or elbows. Instead, I hit my knuckle on the wall.

"Owww!" I cried as I held my sore hand. This was all so unfair. I just wanted to finish the goddamn puzzle. And maybe laminate it. Maybe frame it. So that people can love it forever. I collapsed onto my knees and wept.

Johnny, still covered in seagull webbed-feet barf, crawled over to me, humming.

"Gentle hands, Johnny. Big sister is crying." Mama showed him how to rub my back. He hit my back. I cocooned myself by tucking my knees into my chest. I just didn't have it in me to fight him.

"Gentle! Gentle. See?" Mama showed him again how to rub my back. Johnny settled into a slap–caress down my back. I wanted to stay mad, but he leaned his head against my shirt. His humming on my back felt good.

That night, after Johnny was already asleep, Mama sat beside my bed and surprised me with a Forever Box. It looked familiar.

"This is your medicine box."

"Not anymore. I will find another place for my sage. This is yours now."

I ran my fingers over the simple wood structure, now covered in marker bubble letters spelling out my name. "This is your Forever Box. No one can touch it. You can put your most important things inside there. Johnny won't touch it. I won't touch it. Daddy won't touch it."

"You promise?"

"I promise."

I gave the naked lady lighter a couple more flicks and placed it next to the paintbrushes that Victor left behind.

Last summer, before we were evicted from the community housing townhome complex because of Daddy's gambling, it seemed holes were being burned into the entire neighbourhood. First there were holes burning into the face of Mitchell next door. Then there were holes burning into the faces of his friends who came over. They all looked like evil bowling balls. I wondered how they could drink without it leaking through their cheeks. These white trash folks would gather in the dark corners of the complex, moving between raucous laughter and clandestine whispers. Money exchanged hands. Fistfights erupted and dissolved. Night after night, it was like watching your favourite show. We didn't need cable, which we didn't have anyway. Or a television. And when a hole was burned right through Mitchell's front teeth, Mama understood that meth was a bigger problem than the usual Scarborough grow ops. Weed made houses mouldy; meth made houses blow up. And that's exactly what happened.

Richard, a neighbourhood boy who seemed to be eternally on his too-small bicycle, circled around the stretcher on which Mitchell sat, toothless grin and all. Mitchell's skin was burned to a crisp. His eyebrows were crusty and patchy. Richard circled and circled as he sucked on his lollipop.

"Can you, like, stop? You're making me dizzy, man."

Richard kept circling.

As the cops slowly drove out of our cul-de-sac crowded with nosy people, Victor caught their eye. He was just returning from painting his mural along the Orton Park Bridge.

Victor was a tree. Standing at six feet, two inches, Johnny saw him as a climbing gym. In the mornings, Johnny waited for Victor to walk past our door, pulling his paint and brushes in a red wagon.

"Hello, little mister," Victor would say as Johnny stepped onto his feet, face to face. They would walk together, Johnny the height of Victor's massive muscular legs. Victor would hold his arms out in a T-shape and let Johnny hang like a monkey.

"You sure you don't mind?" Mama said to Victor. He would just smile.

"Okay, little mister," Victor would say, twisting closed the paint bottles that Johnny had loosened open. "I've gotta go."

Victor was the kind of neighbourhood kid who, when he sketched in his book, everyone stopped their jump rope to witness. Dandelion wishes flew across his pages. Old ladies smiled under the stroke of his pencil. He let me rest my cheek on his bicep while he scratched away on the paper portraits of the people sitting across from him. Maurie, the bus driver. Ada, the palm reader. Cindy, the puppy mill lady. They sat obediently on his green plastic stool, smirking at their chance to be immortalized by his grace.

"Quiet down, you bitch!" Cindy said to her prize mutt, Eunice, whose teats hung long and sad, dragging on the concrete from litter after litter. "I swear to God, she thinks she's a queen or something."

People missed him when he got his grant to paint the Orton Park Bridge. I still remember him and his black shaven head looking up at a pair of sneakers suspended by its laces on a high wire. He looked between the sneakers and the expanse of forest below the bridge. Back and forth. Then he looked at the traffic driving past, at the squares of concrete interlocked together to make the bridge.

"See that, Sylvie?" he said to me, his large palm a hat on my tiny head. "Those squares need pictures."

The same summer, he got accepted to OCAD University, and he began painting beautiful images on the bridge. Hands of different colours, their fingers interlacing. Food being shared amongst mothers and their children. He even painted a picture of himself holding Johnny way up high to the sun. That one was my favourite, although I wished it was me in the painting.

That night, when Mitchell's meth operation blew up, a cop locked eyes with Victor on his way back from the bridge.

"Step to the side, sir." I had never seen Victor turn himself off like that. His eyes went blank, and he did exactly as he was told. I could see the cops unscrewing the tops of his paint bottles and smelling the contents, looking at his brushes. They frisked him rigorously. They kept going between their car and Victor, over and over. Victor was arrested.

For what, we still do not understand. He was just painting. The granting body that employed his talents to revitalize the bridge never spoke on his behalf. Because of his arrest, it became impossible for him to land a job to support his schooling.

"Hey, did ya hear about Victor?"

"Can you believe that? And he was living right here under our noses."

"He was always a bit sneaky, that one."

By September, he was back at our housing complex, sketching in his book. In it, he drew bridges.

Slutty Christy wasn't into playing much. I thought, since she was so young, she would be. But she set me straight when we first crossed paths in the common area.

The common area was filled with a variety of second hand furniture. Secrets were revealed in the folds of these 1980s-style sofas. Key chains from unknown places. Important notes scribbled onto pieces of worn paper never to be found again. I was sifting through my found treasures when Christy walked in. Her arms were stories in tattoos, a map to the person she once was, a person who hung out in dark corners looking for a way out, now walking the straight and narrow.

"Whatcha doing?" She looked at her cigarette box and saw one last fag. She put it in her mouth without lighting it as a way of deciding what to do next.

"I got treasures," I said shyly, placing a key chain from Hawaii in my pocket, destined for my Forever Box.

"So? Whatcha got for me today?" Christy poured herself a cup of coffee and sat down on the leather sofa that seemed to exhale under her weight.

This is when she wanted me to tell her stories. She knew I was good at it. Since there wasn't any cable at the shelter, she relied on me for the good times.

"Did you hear about the orangutan at the zoo that tried to swim away?"

"No way. At this here zoo?"

"Yup. The Toronto Zoo."

I began.

"When I was but a wee thing, I remember my mother telling me the tale of the long hairs. She said that if I stood close enough to them without pulling at their fur with my curious paws, I could smell the jungle."

Christy took the cigarette from her mouth and leaned in. She liked the story.

"I sat there sucking on her long leathery boobs while she told me where I came from. Where we had all come from. Even with cameras flashing or kids tapping on the window, I could see it. I could see the rainforest. On and on, with no nets, our long arms grabbing branch to branch.

"That is why, my mother explained, the long hairs had such sad, low cheeks. They weren't fooled by the fake habitat."

"Holy shit," said Christy, patting my back. "You are so freakin' smart, Sylvie. Is this monkey—"

"Orangutan—"

"Is this orangutan a girl or a boy?"

"Girl. For weeks the zoo waited patiently to confirm if I was a girl or boy. Just the slightest touch to the ends of my mom's orange fur made her so angry. She sure was protective. If she could kill with one hand while holding me in the other, she would. Then again, if she could have kept her eyes open instead of falling asleep from those pills the zookeepers gave her that day, she would have been here."

"What?!" Christy stood up suddenly, scratching at her tattoos. "Where did her mom go?"

"The San Diego Zoo. She got transferred."

Just as I was about to explain, Mama came in, looking disapprovingly at Slutty Christy.

Mr George was in charge of me one day during one of my dad's hospital visits, so I waited in the hallway of the shelter near his room, the door ajar, listening to him cough his lungs out. I tried to peer in, to see if he coughed phlegm out of his mouth or his throat hole. I rocked back and forth trying to peek inside into his business. I rocked back and forth until suddenly I was inside the room. I never got used to the smell of old man in there. Like sweet and sour. Like crushed pills and dried spit.

His hand gestured toward me, telling me to wait. We were on our way to the dollar store, me with a shiny loonie I had found at the bus shelter the other night. I was good at finding loose change.

I wished I was like those white kids whose grandparents carted them around on one of those scooters. I saw one once, at the Food Basics. Some chubby white boy with red hair just sitting there on his grandpa's lap, choosing whatever he wanted off the shelves and placing it in the front basket.

Only, Mr George wasn't even my grandpa. He just held my wrist gently but tightly with his weathered hands and walked as slow as a sloth to East Side Crossing strip plaza. It took forever. I looked closely at his scar. It looked like a pink tree starting between his fingers and running down the back of his wrists. I imagined he had been dragged once, accidently or not. I enjoyed when he held me using his left hand, so I could listen to the ticking of his old watch, much too large for his wrist. Maybe a long time ago, it fit him. When he needed both hands, he looped my finger around the side belt buckle of his Wrangler jeans.

We arrived at the dollar store, and its smell of plastic and packaged goods drove me wild with excitement. Right at the entrance, we pushed past a white lady wearing a muumuu and drinking a pop. Mr George slowly guided me up and down every aisle. Paper plates. Clay pottery you can paint yourself. Spray bottles. The possibilities were endless, with this loonie sitting in my sweaty palms.

I explored the cosmetics aisle. Lipsticks that smelled like playdough. Shampoos that smelled like car wash. Flower-printed shower caps. Camo-printed do-rags. In the middle of the aisle was the Super Secret section. I called it "Super Secret" because the ladies who went there always looked left and right to see if anyone was watching. I just rolled my eyes hard to the side so that Mr George couldn't tell I was curious. Mama told me condoms are socks for boy's penises, to keep them from getting girls pregnant. They don't look like socks to me, though. They look like Halloween candies in wrappers. Next to the condoms were boxes of pregnancy tests. Made sense to me. I imagined that if you bought dollar store-quality condoms you'd need dollar-store-quality pregnancy tests. Just as we were passing the nail polishes, the shelf shook, and bags of cotton pads rained down on my head.

It was the white lady in the muumuu. She pushed some man wearing a UFC bandana and a leather jacket into the shelf again. Boxes with images of smiling Black women in shower caps came tumbling down.

The lady managed to throw him down and began pushing into his face with every word. "I ... told ... you! She's ... gone! She ... left! Can't do nothing ... about it, asshole!"

"Get off me, you fat pig!" She held him down between her legs. He was clumsy. Maybe drunk. His punches were weak.

"That's a nice massage you're giving me, fuckface."

Mr George, knowing a good Scarborough fight when he sees one (and knowing the possibility of either party carrying guns), casually turned on his heels and led me to the back of the store while the fight continued. He held my wrist and crouched down. He waved his hand in his old man way for me to do the same, so I did. We were like those soldiers you see in war movies, hiding in the jungle, only we were hiding in the kids' toy section. Dart boards. Rattles. Pretend guitars. Light up yo-yos.

Over the PA system, we heard "Can the manager come to the front, please?" The cashier was in hysterics. The police sirens were already blaring. The customers still lined up, waiting to make their purchases.

"What? You can't ring me through?" said a man with a basket of party favours and balloons.

"Not now, sir." The cashier seemed torn between the growing lineup and the police officers who were entering the premises.

"But it's my niece's birthday party. We gotta get going. I don't give a rat shit about this fist fight. This is the most pitiful fight I've ever seen." The rest of the lineup began to chime in.

"Come on!"

"If we have cash, can we just leave it on the counter?"

"The police are here now. Just ring us through!"

From the back of the store, the manager emerged in a cloud of marijuana smoke from his hot-boxed office, his eyes half closed.

"Okay, everyone. Let's stay calm. Nobody panic," he said, trying desperately to look sober. Everyone stopped to look at the manager, baked as hell, his man bun high atop his head.

By the time the muumuu lady and bandana man were handcuffed and escorted out, I had decided on a light-up yo-yo for my purchase. Mr George and I calmly waited in line like everyone else, as if nothing happened. Just another day in Scarborough. As the lady in front of us said, with one hand pushing her cart full of crayons and Do-It-Your-self birdhouses while the other patted her hair weave, "Drama!"

CORY

A Black woman stood outside Everyting Taste Good Caribbean restaurant as Cory and Laura were walking past on their way to the No Frills grocery store. A hair net enveloped what seemed to be a perfect coif, and her stained apron covered her wide hips. She looked directly at Cory and he stiffened, wondering what she was going to ask for.

"You want free chicken?" she asked, to his surprise. She held out a vacuum-packed bag of eight perfectly good chicken legs. "It's curry." A bucket of similar bags labelled "Cow Heel," "Chicken Pelau," and "Curry Goat" sat at her feet. Diminishing ice cubes swam about in the bucket.

"Excuse me?"

She looked him up and down. "They're spicy."

Just as Cory was about to grab the bag from her, her cellphone rang. She reached into her apron to retrieve it.

"Yes? Uh-uh ... Yes ... Well, I'm out here right now giving it all away before the expiration date."

Cory stared longingly at the bag of chicken in her hands, now cocked on her hip like a baby. His stomach grumbled. The chicken would shave a big chunk off his grocery bill this week. More money for other things, like ciggies and beer.

She continued her phone conversation as if Cory and Laura weren't even there. "Yeah, the freezer system is still warm as an armpit ... Must've been out all night. All the meat was soft and wet ... No ... My dimwitted cousin can't repair the thing until next week."

Cory shifted his weight from foot to foot, wondering if the woman would give up the chicken or not. He flashed a look at Laura who was listening carefully to the woman on the phone. The woman reached into the pocket of her apron for a plastic bag just as a young Black boy opened the door to the restaurant.

"Speaking of dimwitted, here's my nephew ..."

"Auntie Winsum? I don't know how to change the paper roll for the receipts."

Her face contorted into a look of disgust. "I am on the phone, Melvin! Can't you see these kind people waiting for chicken?" She gestured to Cory and Laura as if they were royalty. "Just go get the masking tape and put up the decorations. I will be there in a moment."

Melvin grinned at Cory and Laura, then headed back into the restaurant.

With her phone still set between her shoulder and cheek, the woman spread an Oldham's Wholesale plastic bag wide and placed the vacuum-packed chicken inside, then wiped her wet hands on her apron. Just as she was about to handle the chicken to Cory, she placed it back on her hip. "I'm telling you, this is the last time I hire family to work here. I don't care if he is studying culinary arts at Centennial College. How about a diploma in common sense?" She laughed at her own joke and glanced sideways at Cory, who was glaring at her. Winsum kissed her teeth and finally handed him the bag.

As they walked away, Laura looked back at the skeleton and mock tombstone décor on the restaurant's window.

"Daddy?" Laura asked quietly.

"Hurry up!"

"Daddy?"

"Come on. Pick up the pace. Once word spreads about their freezer, this entire place will be flooded with niggers."

He turned to find his kiddo staring up at him, not knowing what to say.

"What is it, Laura Loo?"

"I need a Halloween costume."

"Well, what do you need that for?" Cory asked, rain making crystals on his eyelashes.

"For Halloween."

Cory sat by the supplies shelf in the literacy centre, his eyes wandering between Laura, eating Cheerios, and the bag of clothes labelled "free for the taking" in indelible marker. Surely there had to be something in there.

"Are you okay, Cory?"

Oh great. It's her again. Cory turned his gaze from the plastic bag toward Ms Hina.

"I think ... I think Laura might need some spare pants. Just spare pants. I think she sat in some milk. I'll clean them and bring them back tomorrow."

"She seems to like the fairy costume. That green one over there with the wings."

Ms Hina pointed to the wooden shelf standing at a tilt, its screws loose and two of its seven hooks pointed upside down. On it was the coveted fairy costume, wings and all, in a stiff tulle mess.

"I think the skirt would go down to her knees to cover the stain."

She knows there's no stain, but she's playing along. They're all so sneaky. She knows what I'm looking for, Cory thought to himself, knowing, had she not intervened, he'd be slipping a Teenage Mutant Ninja Turtles T-shirt on his daughter and calling it a day.

Had it been the nineties all over again, Cory would have already taken a bat to the centre, like he took a bat to those tables at the Scarborough Town Centre food court. Those towelheads didn't see it coming, it was so funny. Had it been the good ol' days, Ms Hina would have known her place just by seeing his shaved head. Back then, Peter, who made all the decisions, decided the lot of them would go into the mall to scare a few folks and take their food. Kill two birds with one stone. They got to scare the shit out of a bunch of Pakis, and they got to be fed. Because God knows, they were hungry. By the end of the night, the gang of four gangly teens were clinking beer bottles to toast a job well done. One wallet with enough cash to buy booze and cigarettes. A half-eaten poutine. A bucket of KFC chicken.

Peter took a swig of beer, then rubbed Cory's newly shaven head like a proud father—maybe like a father—Cory wouldn't know. It just felt good. "Next time we raid, we'll have enough money to get you some ink. You want a tattoo like mine?" Peter rolled up his sleeve to reveal an Iron Cross on his forearm.

Cory rubbed his head, feeling his hair, now greasy and overgrown. Peter's voice, a fleeting echo. Cory was an adult now, no longer a homeless teen, and Ms Hina was facing him with a kind smile on her face.

"You're more than welcome to take the costume, Cory."

He hated hearing his name. The same name as the dad he never knew. He snatched the costume off the rack feeling foolish and clumsy. *Who did she think she was, telling him what to do?*

Ms Hina started storytime with all the children sitting cross-legged.

"*Brown Bear Brown Bear, what do you see?*" Ms Hina and the other rug rats began reciting in their singsong way.

Cory nudged Laura, her nose and tongue wiping the bottom of the bowl for any remaining milk. She got up from the table and pulled up her pants. Cory took the empty bowl and tossed it into the sink.

"Let's go," he said, putting on Laura's My Little Pony backpack. "I fucking hate this book."

LAURA

It was lunch time, and Laura held the magic letter *h* in her hand. Every letter makes a sound. Letters together make a word. Words together make a story. While she waited for the school's side doors to open so she could sneak in, she reviewed in her head all the words she would tell Ms Hina.

"Happy." As in "Happy Birthday," which Mrs Landau and all her classmates sang to her on October 2. Everyone looked at her, clapping and singing. She did not know it was her birthday. She got to wear a birthday crown and got a Happy Birthday pencil from Principal Sankiewicz.

"Halloween." As in Halloween costume, which Ms Hina let Laura borrow. It was a bit tight around the crotch, but if Laura spun around fast enough, the skirt lifted up and made a spaceship circle around her waist.

"Have." As in have and have-not. Clara, the snobby girl, told Laura that Rouge Hill Public School is a have-not school.

"Health." As in health card, which Daddy stood in a long lineup to get for Laura. It finally came in the mail. On it, her birthday was clearly printed "October 2, 2005."

A teacher exited the premises through the side door, struggling with the zipper on their fall coat. Laura snuck in. She made her way to Ms Hina's room, her tummy grumbling.

"Did you have lunch?" Ms Hina was sorting plastic pretend food into pretend grocery carts. Several toddlers took turns going through a tent tunnel, laughing. In a corner, a caregiver changed a baby's diaper. Laura shook her head. Ms Hina went to the cupboard and grabbed a granola bar and a banana. She handed them to Laura with a smile. "Does this look like something you'd like?" Laura smiled back and exchanged the food with the foam letter in her hand.

"You remembered. Okay, let's hear what words you came up with."

Laura put her palm to her mouth, to feel the exhale of air with every word. "Huh–huh–happy. Huh–huh–have. Huh–huh–Halloween. Huh–huh–health."

"Good job," Ms Hina put up her hand. "High-five. See, that starts with *h*, too!" Laura high-fived her. Ms Hina went back to the cabinet and grabbed another foam letter. This time it was the letter *u*.

"This is the letter *u*, and it makes this sound: uh–uh–up." She placed it in Laura's hand. Magic. "Okay, off you go."

Laura ran down the hallway, giggling.

"Hey, slow down, miss."

BING

In the Philippines, it is customary to trace someone's foot onto a piece of paper, cut it out, then go shoe shopping without the shoeless person needing to come. I always found this practice bewildering. Why not bring the person along? How accurate can a paper cut-out be for finding footwear? But by and by, Ma did this for the family, and the shoes always fit perfectly.

The same goes for Filipinos and shopping for pants. Why try them on when you can simply wrap the waist of the desired slacks around your neck? Why bother reading the sizing label on a stack of socks when you can wrap the socks around your fist?

It was only when I found the Ziploc bag containing the tracings of my father's feet that I felt his absence. The same indelible ink used to label the bag "Pa's shoes, Florsheim, size 10" was used to make the palimpsest that was no longer Daddy. A shadow of a shadow of a shadow of a whisper.

My tears were finally unleashed in the dramatic fashion of Filipino mourning, like lacerating a boil so the infection could heal.

I remember as a young child watching, for the first time, the novena being recited in honour of my uncle's death. The repetition, the sorrow expressed in every rosary bead, the pouty-faced Mother Marys at every turn of the page in the novena prayer book were enough to make one wail. And that was the point. Just short of screaming at the deceased, we were, as a community, telling Tito Ferdie to leave us. Leave us behind, look forward into God's embrace, and walk. Walk far away from us. Even though, in our hearts, we wanted the person to be alive, we knew that if we didn't encourage the spirit to pass into the afterlife, it would linger, and it would worry about us.

So I cried. I cried until my cries turned to wails. The louder, the better. Go, Daddy. Go and walk. To the other side where you will feel better. It felt right to treat his parting like a death. It was the death of everything I knew.

I admit to having fleeting fantasies of becoming the first Filipino country music star. This is, of course, second to my fantasy of becoming a saint. But since Ma informed me one has to be dead to become a saint, a country music star seems to be the best bet.

In my *kamiseta* and underwear, in front of the washroom mirror, my dream comes true. Under the glow of the overhead lighting, I sing the lyrics to the song that my daddy would hear. His son. No longer chubby and ugly, but handsome and thin.

He is sitting in a bar, having recovered from being mentally ill, now earning an honest wage and looking with honest regret at his past and everything he had done to us. Then, on the bar's television screen, I appear, his handsome and thin son Bing, now known by his stage name, Boy Delacruz, singing to his long-lost father.

The camera catches a glimpse, underneath my Stetson hat, of my misty eyes. The quivering lip behind my adult stubble. I speak, my voice low and sombre: "This one, this song is special. It goes out to my daddy. Wherever you are."

My daddy almost loses his balance as he stands up from the bar stool.

"That's my son! That's my son! And he's so handsome and thin!"
And then I sing.

> We'll leave the light on outside our home
>
> So in the darkest nights you'll know you're not alone
>
> We'll leave the light on outside our door
>
> Daddy, that's what family's for.

The sighting, of course, leads to our reunion. The reunion leads
to our doing the things we always did before: food court meals, ice
cream trucks, see-saws.

It is a splendid fantasy, complete with American Idol judge re-
marks, love affairs, unwanted paparazzi, you name it.

But another fantasy is brewing. And it makes me think I am
abandoning my daddy each time I imagine it.

It was Halloween, and Ma compromised on my costume.

"It's too cold to be a saint." She explained about Canadian cold,
which was two-years new to me.

So she allowed me to be a priest. It was cheap: one piece of white
masking tape on my black turtleneck. It was warm: black fleece pants
and an oversized overcoat, making me look like a plush version of
a missionary. She used Dippity-do to slick my hair to the side and
drew a moustache and beard on my face with her eyeliner.

"Now your name is Father Bernard." Ma smell-kissed my forehead and handed me my lunch.

I took the lunch bag full of stinky, half-warm chicken adobo and
rice, both of us laughing in our apartment hallway. "*Saint* Bernard!"

Ma's finishing touch for my costume were my props. A black

paper-covered notebook to look like a bible. A sleeve of haw flakes, to play communion.

Before bell at the literacy centre, I told Sylvie to line up. Ma helped me open the haw flakes, then ceremoniously gave them to me. "*Sige na,* go play," she said with a smile and simultaneous roll of her eyes.

I got a good whiff of the Asian market's fishy smell still on the paper sleeve; the flakes themselves were a hybrid scent of raisins and brown sugar.

I held one round flake in my hand between finger and thumb.

"Body of Christ."

Sylvie stared at me, perplexed.

"That's when you say 'Amen.'"

"Ohhh ..." she said.

I instructed her to keep her arms folded in front of her and to stick her tongue out so I could place the "communion wafer" on it. She obliged in fits of giggles. Then she stepped aside and behind her was Laura, the girl from my building, dressed in a fairy costume.

"Can I have some?"

"Sure. Stick your tongue out."

Round and round they walked in a rotating line, until almost all of my haw flakes were finished. I made sure I took a wafer after every repetition. I knew priests did not do this. They served communion after eating only one wafer themselves, but the haw flakes were so yummy, I couldn't help it.

"Where did all the Jesus go?" Laura said.

"It's finished," I said, scrunching the sleeve before putting it into the garbage bin beside mountains of Halloween chocolate bar wrappers.

Just before the bell rang for us to head to class, Sylvie's mom pulled out a red lipstick to make Sylvie look like a Raggedy Ann doll. Her mom had managed to find an apron and had tied Sylvie's hair into two braids. The final touch was the makeup. Her mom sat down and pulled her in and wrapped her legs around Sylvie to keep her from moving while she drew circles on her cheeks, then smudged them into a garish blush.

"You want some too?" I thought Sylvie's mom was talking to me, and as I stepped forward, Laura passed me.

"Sure!" Laura replied. Laura got the full glam treatment. Since she was a fairy, she got both rosy cheeks and ruby red lips.

"All you need is lipstick!" Sylvie's mom giggled. She shook her head at the sight of the two girls. "Goddamn it, my lipstick is almost all used up. You both look like tramps."

I was suddenly sad, feeling the grease of the painted-on beard. I wanted lipstick, too.

The weight of my mother's arm sloped across my shoulders. It was firm. A fence. I knew she had seen me take a step forward when the lipstick was offered. Her downwards gaze at me made me feel so ashamed. Then, to my surprise, she bent down, kissed me on the forehead, and whispered in my ear. "Not here."

She knew. The pairs of heels that were out of place in her closet. The worn-down lipstick. The dresses hanging lopsided on their hangers.

I looked up and saw her smiling at me, tears welling in her eyes. "Another time. Not here."

DAILY REPORT

October 31, 2011

Facilitator: Hina Hassani

Location: Rouge Hill Public School

Attendance:

Parent/Guardian/Caregiver	Children (one per line please)
Cory Mitkowski	Laura Mitkowski
Edna Espiritu	Bernard Espiritu
Helen McKay	Finnegan Everson
	Liam Williams
	Sebastian Dennis
	Chloe Smith
Fern Donahue	Paulo Sanchez
	Kyle Keegan
Marie Beaudoin	Sylvie Beaudoin
	Johnny Beaudoin
Lily Chan	Jennifer Chan
	Aiden Chan
Yanna Knowles	Reese Knowles
Sonia DiSorono	Luka DiSorono
Anna Maria De Souza	Winston Dunst
	Benjamin Tate
	Paula Santiago
Pamela Roy	Evan Roy
	Yanna Roy
	Tasha Roy

Notes:

Halloween was a blast despite the rain. Lots of kiddos in cute costumes. The Chan family had them in matching dim sum outfits. Each kid had a hat with pork buns. So adorable! We made some pretzels shaped in the letters spelling "Halloween." Not that the kids knew. They ate the letters before we could even decorate them. Oh well.

Mrs Rhodes has been included in our conversation around Bing and his possible giftedness designation. I have forwarded them my thoughts for his assessment and will support his mother, Edna, through this possible transition and her decision making. He comes to me for extra work since, he tells me, he's not challenged enough in Mrs Finnegan's class. I usually give him story writing prompts, which he hands me the next day with ease. Today, though, he and Sylvie asked to make friendship bracelets. I gave them two colours of yarn, and they went to work. What was amazing is that they noticed Laura watching from the side, and they let her join in. It was lovely to watch. All of this strategizing around Laura, and she integrated herself into the group.

Weekly supplies requested:

2% milk	three bags, please
Cheerios	one box
Shreddies	one box
apples	one bag
bananas	two bunches

Jane Fulton <jfulton@ontarioreads.ca>
November 1, 2011
10:22 a.m. (9 hours ago)
To <hhassani@ontarioreads.ca>

Hi, Hina:
Halloween sounded like a hoot!
Judging by your attendance, you had only
seventeen children and their caregivers/
parents. Not to alarm you, but usually Halloween (or any holiday for that matter) is
a big attendance day for most centres in
the province. It's not surprising if there
are thirty plus people there. Do you have
a clue why your numbers were the way they
were? I know the centre is relatively new.
But did you have the chance to flyer the
neighbourhood, as I had mentioned?
Also, I was watching the CBC the other
day and noticed you in the crowds at some
Indian cultural event with the NDP. Was
that you? I just wanted to check. We have
a right to stand by our political opinions, but I must caution you that the centres pride themselves on being no-politics
zones.
Especially as the centres are the pride
and joy of the Liberal Party, I want to
ensure your NDP sentiments won't hurt the
neutrality of your workplace. You can imagine how the simple things we do every day
can make a statement—be it what we say or

how we dress (your hijab, for example)—and
how they may affect the community's opinion of you and what the centre can provide.
Would love to know your thoughts about how
you plan to keep these two worlds separate!
   Lastly, I am concerned about your grocery
bill. I notice lots of requests for cereals
and milk. Just checking that people aren't
expecting a breakfast program out of our
beloved centres.
Jane Fulton, MSW
Supervisor, Ontario Reads Program
*Reading is a way for me to expand my mind,
open my eyes, and fill up my heart.*
   —Oprah Winfrey

Me <hhassani@ontarioreads.ca>
November 1 2011
1:15 p.m. (3 hours ago)
To Jane Fulton <jfulton@ontarioreads.ca>

Hello, Jane:
Thanks for your feedback.
I will happily start flyering during my free
time once I better understand how exactly I
will be compensated for this labour. I hope
you understand that spending my free time
with my family is very important to me. I
would love to discuss with you, and perhaps
our union representative, ways we can trou-
bleshoot this situation so that it is fair
for all concerned.

The footage you saw on the CBC was of my cousin Raj, who is running as a New Democratic Party candidate in the West Rouge district. Perhaps you were confused, since there were many South Asians in attendance. We are all very proud of Raj and stand by his skills. The "Indian cultural event" you mentioned was actually a fundraiser for Because I am a Girl, which is an international movement to end gender inequality. Again, my personal time is my own and is very important to me—as is my hijab. You can rest assured that my dangerous NDP views won't be heard at the centre. ☺

Sincerely,

Hina Hassani, Facilitator

Ontario Reads Program, Rouge Hill Public School

PART TWO

WINTER

The Rouge River is frozen still and quiet. Grandfather Heron hides.

At Warden Station
Despite the cold, a lineup builds at a café, as people wait for their
Jamaican beef patties, a delicacy sandwiched between coco bread
buns. People relish its heat in their hands and the steam across their
faces.

At the corner of Markham and Eglinton
Lucky 88 Asian Market is busy. Brown and Black folks of all sorts
take a number and wait for the butcher to cut their choice meat.
Whole goat. Oxtail. Beef tongue.

SYLVIE

It was an indoor recess, because of the snowstorm. Bing and I were busy with the comic book we were writing and drawing together.

"This is for you, Bernard." Mrs Finnegan placed an envelope on Bing's desk, then patted him on the back, like he'd earned it. "Don't forget to put that in your backpack. Best to put it in there now, don't you think?"

Bing obeyed. He got up from our desks and headed to his bag, which was hanging on the wall. Standing there, he opened the envelope and read the letter inside. When he came back, he looked different.

"What's that for?" I asked him.

"Don't you know?" Clara tilted her head at me with a look of disgust. "This is the year they start testing everyone for the gifted program."

I looked at Bing to see if this was the truth, but he refused to look back at me. He just pretended to colour in our comic book. I could tell he was pretending because he was using his green marker over and over on the same patch of paper.

"My dad says I'm gifted in other ways. Some people are book smart, but I'm art smart. That's why I'm part of the children's choir. He says that kids in the gifted program are socially awkward, but arts kids are social butterflies." She snapped her pencil case closed like she was some lawyer on TV closing her briefcase. I wanted to shut that pencil case closed on her fingers, I hated her so much.

The school bell rang the end of indoor recess.

"Awwww!' the kids all said together. As everyone began putting away puzzles and board games, I tapped Bing on the shoulder.

"Can I please see the letter Mrs Finnegan gave you?"

"It's for Ma."

"Please?"

"I can't forget it in my bag. I can't take it out now. It's very important."

"You read what was inside. Why can't you tell me?" I waited. He looked at his shoes. "Are you in trouble?"

"No."

"If you don't show me, I'm going to tell your ma that you took a bottle of that slutty pink nail polish to paint your binder cover." Bing's eyes widened in fear.

"Sylvie Beaudoin. Bernard Espiritu. Please, sit down. Indoor recess is over now." Mrs Finnegan looked down at both of us over her reading glasses. I realized everyone was seated at their desks.

For the rest of the day, I had wished we could play Cursive Writing. It wasn't even a game, but I really wanted to watch Bing's pen gracefully move about the paper.

I tried to write a letter with that same writing. I wanted to tell him I was sorry for getting him in trouble. I wanted to know if he was okay. And if he wasn't okay, I wanted him to know he could tell me that, too. But I knew my cursive writing was illegible to him.

After school, I saw Mama outside. Johnny was out of the stroller, and an old television set sat in his place. Mama was twirling the cord into a perfect knot as I approached her. I was so embarrassed and hoped Clara wouldn't see us. That snooty bitch.

"You won't believe it!" she said, while shooing away Johnny's prying fingers from the TV's clicking knobs. "It was just sitting there outside of National Thrift waiting for someone to take it. Someone left it there as a donation, but National Thrift was closed. I feel so damned lucky!"

When we got home, Mama plugged the set in. It had a large knob to change the channels. She clicked it back and forth and found only one channel that worked. Black and white images emerged from the squiggles on the screen.

"You see him over there? When you serve him his martini, hand him this note, see? You have approximately ten minutes to deliver it. After that, the invisible ink will be unreadable."

"But how will he know what it says? It's gibberish!"

"It's not gibberish, Charlie. It's in code. I'll explain it later. Now, get out there and serve your country!"

Watching these spies disguised as waiters, my eyes twinkled. I knew exactly what to do.

Two days later, I was ready. With the letter in my pocket, I searched the costume bin at the literacy centre. No trench coat, but Ms Hina did lend me a pair of sunglasses.

"Nice glasses, Sylvie," said Clara sarcastically. She pursed her lips at me. I took the glasses off and shoved them into my desk. So much for the disguise.

With my hand still in my desk, I searched the mess of orange peels and crumpled granola bar wrappers until I found a pencil. My strategy was to use the pencil sharpener screwed to the doorframe near Bing's desk, then to casually drop the letter on his desk on the way back to mine. Bing would see the truth, Mrs Finnegan would see nothing, and I would have a sharp pencil.

Mrs Finnegan began her lesson on Venn diagrams by drawing two large, overlapping circles on the chalkboard. She scribbled a stick figure with a cowboy hat on the right-hand side of the diagram. "Let's say we have two farmers." On the left-hand side, she scribbled another stick figure, with something in his mouth.

"Is he smoking?" said Hakim with a giggle. Everyone laughed.

"No!" Mrs Finnegan always seemed to be on the edge of screaming. "That's straw. The farmer's chewing it." She turned to face us, reaching for her coffee cup. She took a drink and a deep breath and turned back to the chalkboard.

This was my chance. I got up and began to whistle as I strolled along the row. Casual.

"Since both Farmer Smith and Farmer MacDonald have sheep, we will put the word *sheep* in this middle part—" Mrs Finnegan broke off and looked around, confused. "What is that sound? Hakim, is that you?"

I stopped whistling and rushed over to the sharpener. No more time for casual. Eagerly, I turned the hand crank. Grind, scratch, click.

Mrs Finnegan continued over the noise. "But since Farmer Smith is the only one who has chickens, can anyone tell me where we should write the word *chickens*?"

I watched Bing. He looked so bored. "Sylvie?" Mrs Finnegan and the entire class was looking at me. "Do you think your pencil is sharp enough?"

I looked down. My pencil was the size of a toothpick, thanks to my daydreaming. Everyone looked back at the chalkboard. It was now or never.

My heart pounded as I approached Bing's desk. I focused on the silhouette of his undershirt beneath his button-up shirt, on the icing sugar rolls of baby powder and sweat between his neck folds. With great nonchalance, I dropped the wet wipe of a letter, damp from my sweaty palms, on his desk, and kept strolling. I could feel him looking at me but didn't look back. Casual.

I watched his back muscles reconfigure when he realized the letter was in code and had a key. He took a pen from his pencil case, and his muscles changed shape again as he deciphered my letter. Then I watched the muscles reconfigure as he read what I had written:

> *Dear Bing,*
> *You are my best friend.*
> *Love, Sylvie*

At recess, I found Bing hiding in the alcove of the school's back doors. He was sort of staring at the brown brick wall of the school and kicking the concrete, like he was bored. I sat down on the cold grey surface and rested my chin on my bony knees, knowing he wanted to talk.

"I watched my dad put his hand into the frying pan. That's why we're alone now. Ma says he is sick in his head and heart, and it's not his fault. He didn't go to the doctor." Bing was suddenly still. His forehead rested on the brick. "You're my best friend, too."

I looked at him. He had that moon face only fat kids have. Like someone sewed on eyes, a nose, and a mouth too small for such a large surface. I could hear him breathing, the snot getting in the way, the tears flowing. He wiped them away. I gave him the napkin from my pocket that Mama had packed for my lunch that day. It had a bit of pizza sauce left over from the corners of my mouth, but I knew he wouldn't mind. That's what best friends are like.

"Are you going into the gifted program?" I asked, never wanting to let him go.

"I don't know. Mrs Finnegan wants me to get tested. But it's far away."

"You left me hanging, little girl."

Christy's brown hair was newly shaved on one side and the other was draped over her face. She smelled good today. She looked awake and eager. Like last time, she poured herself a cup of black coffee and sat near me and my pile of newly found treasures, this time a note with the words *right on College, left at Bathurst*, as well as a mood ring.

I began.

"My mother did not give me my name. It was given to me by a young girl named Samantha, who scribbled my name onto paper with a purple marker. She folded the paper twice and placed it in a plastic bin. It was a contest to see who would name the new orangutan. The zookeeper shook the bin, then reached her hand inside.

Once she pulled out Samantha's submission, the zookeeper held it up high for all to see. When asked why she chose the name Clementine, Samantha answered, 'Because she's orange, and she's small.' My mother knew what my real name was, though. She whispered it into my ear while I nursed. It was also the last thing she said to me before they took her away to the San Diego Zoo."

"What was it?" Christy interjected.

I whispered it into Christy's ear, the ear next to her shaven head. A secret.

I continued.

"Before I tell you the rest of this story, I have to make it perfectly clear that my mother did not try to drown me, as the newspaper said. She had a funny feeling, is all. Something was speaking to her near the wading pool that surrounded our part of the zoo. Something told her to let me swim. For days she would pace beside the pool, this pool that was meant to keep us from climbing. From escaping. The zookeepers knew we orangutans could climb. Climb anything. Climb a wall of slippery fish covered in Vaseline. Climb a waterfall of spaghetti. But we could not swim."

Christy laughed. Patted me on the head.

"Only my mother knew different. At least, that is what she heard from the water. She tried once to dip her toes in, but couldn't fight the sick feeling in her belly. She didn't like wet fur or cold between her toes. But what about her baby? What would her baby girl know of fear?"

Christy suddenly stood. Her face was red. "No she didn't."

"No she didn't," I reassured her. Christy scratched at her tattoo, flakes hitting the air and sunlight.

"The zookeeper started thinking my mom was acting strange. Her pacing—with a baby girl on her back—made the zookeeper nervous.

"One day, the zookeeper began offering food near the pool. The crowd was taking photos as the long hairs and the rest of my sisters and brothers walked to the edge. Mama didn't care though. She just looked at her reflection in the water. Touch me, the water said. Touch me and be free. She looked at her reflection. At the reflection of the zoo's fake trees and glass ceiling. At the reflection of her child, me, on her back, ready to swim.

"After my mother was taken away, I couldn't stop thinking of the water. I grew old, sitting in the corners, pulling out the fur along my shoulders, dreaming of swimming. For years, I ate from my perch. I slept while people took pictures of me. I sat and watched the sun travel across the ceiling from east to west."

Christy sank down on the leather sofa. An exhale.

"When I began poking holes in my own cheeks, the Painted Box Turtles stopped me.

"'Patience!' they all said together from their wading pool next to my lookout. Their old eyes looked over the surface of their aquarium toward me, through me, in me, as they formed a choir.

"'What is it you dream of?' they finally asked, their beady eyes still while their legs treaded water.

"What the long hairs have seen. Where they come from. Where I belong.

"The choir of turtles turned inwards toward each other and

whispered old whispers. Then they swam away. I beat my chest. I swung from perch to perch. But they were finished."

"'Patience,' they said, their heads rotating like a line of synchronized swimmers. 'Patience.'"

Christy exhaled and patted me on the back. She was done for now.

"I gotta get some ciggies," she explained.

Somewhere between getting ciggies and the budding of the trees, Christy lost interest in the story of Clementine. She let her shaven hair grow in. She began to dog-ear self-help books and quoted from them often.

"When you make a list of all the things you want in the universe, you just say thank you. Not, I want this, I want that." She scribbled on Hello Kitty paper she found in the shelter's arts and crafts room. Using Crayola marker, she wrote the words "Thank you for the king-size bed. Thank you for the window facing the lake.

"You're, like, aligning yourself, you know? Aligning yourself with the energy of these desires. If you say I want this, I want that, the universe will only reflect back to you that you're a person who wants things. Not has things."

She knocked on our door, asking Mama for some medicine to smudge. She told Mama she wanted the Creator to guide her, or something.

"For God's sake. Will that bitch leave me alone already? I don't care if she says she's a quarter Blackfoot. I'm not giving her any more of my damn sage. She can get her own."

I noticed she owned a new cellphone, which she used to text

with her new boyfriend, who bought her the phone. The case of it was a bedazzled star, which Christy picked at between messages.

"Roy made it so I can text him as much as I want," she explained to me once.

While her body grew skinnier, her voice became louder. Between fleeting moments in the common area, I found her in the dark corners of the shelter, texting longingly into her phone, wiping away tears. The next day, she was sunny all over again, showing me the new dress Roy had bought her.

I wanted to tell Christy how the White Handed Gibbons, who were naturally bipedal as well as being excellent climbers and throwers, were instrumental in giving Clementine and the other orangutans pieces of the puzzle. I wanted to tell her how the Painted Box Turtles instructed the White Breasted Water Hens to steal a list of carefully chosen objects. I wanted to tell her that the zoo began to post warnings to their workers of theft after road maps, necklaces, jackets, pens, knives, and clipboards went missing. But Christy wasn't interested anymore. She was too busy waiting for Roy to text her back after last night's fight.

BING

I couldn't stop thinking about Hakim. He was like a wild horse to me. Untamed, he hit girls at random and laughed in the face of guilt, preferring to be sent to the office than to apologize. He had no fear crossing the street without holding an adult's hand. And now, he was kissing all the girls on the playground. He lacked modesty in language and body and was unknowing of the bible, something that I with my Christian sensibility was surprised to adore. His kissing frenzy was the talk of the schoolyard and was fuelling my new fantasies.

"He's so gross!" said Clara, that Twinkie kid, the only girl in school who managed to have a hand-me-down free wardrobe. She was fancy, rich, and white. Of course, Hakim would want to kiss her.

What a liar! I thought to myself but would never say out loud. *I know she likes it. She should be so lucky.* I often imagined the texture of his chapped lips against mine. What it would be like to linger at the bottom of the slide, just the two of us, a puppy pile of budding love. Sharing lunches. Trading carrot sticks for dried mango. Passing notes to each other in class. *Dinner tonight? Yes? No? Maybe?*

Right beside Rouge Hill Public School is a community centre and hockey arena. Every day after school, families with lighter skin and two whole parents with two whole jobs drive to the ice rink for hockey lessons. Out of the minivans, their back windows illustrated with those family stickers: the largest stick figure, a father; the medium-sized one in a skirt, the mother; and so on to show everyone their three healthy children, their cat, their dog, emerge these perfect families, hockey gear and all, their ice skates clinking as they rush inside.

We, the brown kids with one and one-half parents, with siblings from different dads we see only in photos; we who call our grandmothers Mom; we who touch our father's hands through Plexiglas; we wait for their fanfare to be over. We wait through the weekends of extracurricular activity for Mondays, when the Zamboni resurfaces the rink and leaves a pile of chemical-ridden "snow" outside.

This mountain-high remnant of the nuclear family was what we delighted in, mid-winter, climbing to the top in our second-hand sneakers and sliding down on garbage bags. This shadow of the outlines we would never live up to is what we took in handfuls, to throw at each other in fits of laughter and joy.

On one particular Monday, a freezing rainstorm transformed the pile into an icy castle. It took a whopping ten minutes just to ascend the massive thing, what with no grip on our shoes, and only seconds to descend into the chain-link fence. I decided to burrow holes instead, deep into the depths of the snow mountain. I used my gloves, too short to protect my red frostbitten wrists, to dig caverns big enough to fit my chubby body.

It was meditative, creating a space in which I could hear myself breathe. Above me, I could hear the hooligans sliding on the surface as I continued my earnest work below. I turned to find Hakim on his knees, doing the same thing; his burrow had connected with mine.

In this space, we could hear only our breathing, the fabric of our snow pants silent. He looked directly at me. My heart began to pound so hard I could feel it in my earlobes.

He looked up at the low ceiling of snow above our heads. "Did you know that if there are enough people tobogganing above us, this cave will collapse?" We looked at each other. "They won't even hear us scream. They'll just keep tobogganing until sunset. And by then, we'll already be frozen to death." The fog of my breath mixed with his fog. I gulped.

Hakim, still on his knees, crept forward. His wet mittens grabbed hold of my hood, and he kissed me. His cheeks were cold. His nose was snotty. But it was like a movie kiss, with his head turning side to side, his tongue twisting here and there. I was motionless, burning inside, not wanting it to end. Then he pulled away from me suddenly and returned to digging.

I was too busy hearing music in my head to wonder at the hardness under my snow pants. I almost died in the arms of the boy I love, I thought to myself. We almost died doing what was dangerous, forbidden. I didn't need to be a saint any longer. I was a secret-keeper from now on.

CORY

"You ready, kiddo?"

With his elbows resting heavily on the kitchen table, Cory unfolded the orange-coloured paper and read the instructions out loud.

"Hello parents! It's that time again. On December 12, we will be celebrating winter with our annual Carnaval, in the style of our neighbouring province of Quebec. The entire day will be filled with snow-castle building and ice sculptures, and each student will be given a small taste of maple syrup taffy. The students in Mrs Landau's class will be pitching in this year, with their newly learned French vocabulary. Each child is asked to present a sign on which they've illustrated their assigned French term or word associated with Quebec's Carnaval."

The memo ended with a scribble in Sharpie at the bottom of the page. Laura Mitkowski: Bonhomme de neige.

"Bonhom. Duh. Neg. What the hell is that?"

"It means," Laura used her fingers to follow the words, pretending to read, "sss-no-mmm-aaa-nnn."

"Snowman? Is that so? Okay, so let's take inventory, missy." Cory scooped up Laura and placed her in the wicker kitchen chair.

"Cotton balls."

"Check." Laura squished the bag of fluff in her hands.

"White glue."

"Check."

"What's this red string for?"

"He wears this red belt thingy."

Cory spread out the Bristol board that Mrs Landau had enclosed with the supplies.

"Why don't you get started on the cotton balls first?" Cory tore open the bag and emptied it onto the table. "You know how to make a snowman, dontcha?" Laura nodded.

While she got to work, Cory pressed play on the CD player sitting beside the stove. The band English Beat blasted from the speakers. He nodded his head as if obeying to the rhythm. Laura giggled as Cory danced to the cupboard and got a can of Chef Boyardee ravioli. She nodded to the beat too as Cory shimmied to the bottom oven drawer to retrieve a saucepan. Laura giggled some more. "Come on, Laura Loo! Get your head into it! Make your mean face!"

The lyrics came so easily to Cory. He had heard them so many times. In borrowed cars, heading to darkened bridges. In Peter's house, celebrating Cory's first time rolling some Black boy for his shoes. While getting his tattoo, the boys laughing at his tears. While watching Peter be escorted into the back of a cop's car, Peter smirking the entire time.

Dancing in a circle, Cory's eyes fell on Laura's figure-eight snowman shape of cotton balls, but with no glue to adhere it to the board.

He scoffed, "What are you doing? You need to put glue on it first, you retard."

Laura's face blushed.

He paused at the heat rising in his throat.

"Go on," he patted Laura's head jokingly. "Put the glue on first." He grabbed the glue bottle and the lid of a long-lost plastic container. He squeezed the bottle, upside down. The nozzle was not open. Gripping it tightly, he tried to twist it counter-clockwise. Righty-tighty, lefty-loosey. It did not budge. He took the lid off the bottle instead and turned the bottle upside down. Glue poured out, covering the container lid with much too much glue. He threw the bottle across the room into the sink. Laura flinched. Catching himself, he patted her on the head again. Laura flinched.

He went back to the saucepan to stir the ravioli.

"This is fun, isn't it? You're gonna have the best sign in the class." Pasta stuck to the surface of the pan. He turned down the temperature and took a deep breath.

The CD started skipping. He slammed the stop button, and the CD door flew open. He slammed the CD door down. Again. Again. It finally closed. He took a deep breath.

He turned back to Laura to see her silently scooping up handfuls of glue overflowing the container lid. She looked at Cory, her face red. Her hands were frantic, doing the impossible task of picking up liquid with her fingers.

"Stop! Stop! Fucking stop! What the hell are you doing?" Cory grabbed a kitchen towel and began wiping up the mess. "You're making a goddamn snowman, not building the CN tower. Stupid bitch." On his hands and knees, he looked up at Laura. She was holding her knees together and peeing. Glue on her hands. Pee down her legs. She whimpered.

"What the fuck, Laura?! Seriously, what the fuck is wrong with you?" He grabbed her chin and held it, tight enough until it felt good to hurt her. "Look at this mess, look! What is fucking wrong with—

What's that smell?" He whipped around. The ravioli was burning. With a deep belly yell, he threw the pot at the wall near Laura's head. Blackened tomato sauce splattered the top of Laura's hair. Laura froze.

"See what you did? See what you made me do?!" The room was suddenly quiet.

He began to pace the room like a lion in a cage. "I don't know, man. I don't know. Sometimes ... sometimes ..." He used his fingers to twist his lips, trying to find the words. Laura couldn't hear anything. All the switches on her body had suddenly turned off. Her arms were numb, and her throat clenched. Cory continued to pace. "You're good, right? You're okay? You're okay, right?" He began to whimper like a puppy Laura once saw on television. "I don't know, man. I mean ..." He paused and looked pleadingly at Laura. He knelt before her, but her gaze was somewhere far away.

"You know, your mom ... A lot of people thought they knew her when they didn't. They didn't know the Jessica I knew. You know why they put her in a foster home, sweetie?" Cory blinked away fat tears onto his red cheeks; he wiped snot across the gin blossoms on his nose. "Because her grandma, who was supposed to be taking care of her, left her. She told me all of this. Because I was there to listen. She told me everything. She told me she was just a kid, like you, and that old lady tried her hardest to lose her. And on that subway platform, she did just that. The old lady walked fast enough through the crowd that your mom was lost forever. I thought I found her, but I didn't. I thought I found you, but ..." Cory sobbed uncontrollably. Like he was choking. "Now I don't know. I'm just as bad as that old lady, aren't I, Laura. Laura Loo?" Laura was as still as a doll. Her eyes were glassy. Cory, still on his knees, wrapped his arms around her, hoping to feel her hug him back. She remained limp.

"Hit me. Come on, Laura Loo! Hit me!" He took her passive hands and hit his own face. Laura remained limp. Crying, he crawled toward his jacket, got up, and made for the door.

LAURA

It was after Daddy had stormed out, after what little twilight was left in the sky transformed from lavender to darkness, that Laura came out of her stupor. All the switches on her body came back on. She swallowed hard. She blinked even harder, realizing she hadn't in a while. She felt a soreness on her chin. She remembered but didn't remember. The room came into focus. Slowly. The fog dissipated, and the details of the apartment became clearer. Where she was situated within the room became clearer. *This is my body. This is tomato sauce in my hair. These are my legs. I am sitting on the carpet. I am wet. It is dark outside. I am alone, again.*

She removed crust from her eyes. Wiped away guck from the sides of her mouth. Opened and closed her fists. Her tailbone was sore, so she got up and looked at the wet spot underneath her bum. She stared at it for a while. A problem she couldn't solve. She took off her leggings and panties and used them to sop up the moisture. After a few good presses, she felt the carpet with her hand. Good enough. She looked at the stained clothes, wondering where to put them now. She stared at them for a while. A problem she couldn't solve.

As silent as a mouse and still pantless, Laura went to the window of the now dark room to watch the snow fall. It fell as silently as she had travelled across the carpet to the window. That silent window. A street lamp marked the forty-five-degree angle of the falling snow. Down below, Laura saw a woman standing outside the back of the massage parlour smoking a cigarette.

They caught each other's eyes. Both blonde. Both cold. One inside, one outside. One young, the other younger. They waved.

When Laura was living with her mother in a low-rise apartment complex near Kennedy and Eglinton, her two major jobs were to reach for things and to guard the door.

Jessica was out of the house for prolonged periods of time. Sun rising and setting. Rising and setting. All silence. In this silence, Laura made tasks for herself, like drooling into a puddle at the edge of the carpet to see how much drool it would take to make an ocean. Sometimes she played swimming in the bathtub, where she peed to make the water yellow. Sometimes she watched mould grow along loaves of old bread, waiting for it to turn into a forest.

She did not know how to read. So when pieces of paper were slipped underneath the door, she did not know that they were notices from the landlord. She took a pair of shears from the kitchen and began to cut these yellow notices into the shape of a mother duck. The shavings became a nest. Laura imagined it was her duck farm and placed the mama duck on the window ledge to watch it grow and feed on anything Laura could find, be it cotton swabs or hairpins.

"Mama Duck said 'quack, quack, quack, quack,' but none of her five little ducklings came back ..." Laura sang while cutting five eggs out of more yellow notices slipped under the door. She placed them in the shredded paper nest under their two-dimensional mama.

The sun rose and set. Rose and set.

"Five little ducks went out one day, over the hills and far away ..."

Laura happily skipped to the nest, ready for the ducklings to hatch. She used the shears to cut the paper eggs open. Only, there weren't any ducklings inside. Thankfully, at that moment a pink piece of paper slid under the door with big angry letters on it. She cut out five pink ducklings, gave them faces with her mother's ballpoint pen. She placed them underneath their paper mama for warmth. They needed to rest.

The sound of an ambulance drew her to the window, delighted. It meant that a crowd of people were gathering, and perhaps one would wave to her, up on the second floor. They didn't. They were too busy shaking their heads over the bloody body of L, the man who rolled his money in rubber bands and had lots of visitors.

At night, when the rest of the tenants were watching talk shows, Laura took her mother's razor blade and shaved her entire body. She shaved her vulva, which she witnessed her mother do while smoking a cigarette, before leaving on her extended outings. Laura shaved one of her eyebrows and stopped when she clipped her skin.

One day there was a knock at the door. She pulled the step stool over and looked through the peephole. It was Mrs Kamal. Her be-jewelled hijab was a wonderful mystery to Laura, but her mother never let her say hello.

Laura opened the door. The stink from inside made Mrs Ka-mal cringe. She guided Laura to her apartment across the hallway. Food. The sound of Arabic became the soundtrack to Laura's surviv-al. When Mrs Kamal found lice in her hair, Laura was shuffled back to her own home, and the door was closed for good.

Some time. Some time passed. Some time, after Laura used

the last of the toilet paper. Some time, after she decided to eat the mouldy bread. Some time, after she made piles of lice, which she plucked from her own scalp, her mother walked in.

Jessica's hips rotated to and fro, making a beeline to her bed. She resumed her last position, face down, chin touching the saliva stain she had made before leaving the last time. Laura took hold of the bedspread and tucked her sleeping mother in. She found gum in her mother's purse, which she chewed and swallowed to feel weight in her stomach.

One day, after another yellow sheet of paper was slipped underneath the door, Jessica tried to turn the tide. She began to care for neighbourhood kids. They were the kinds of kids with poor brown and Black parents who knew full well that Jessica was unfit to care for their kids, but they had no choice. They couldn't afford anywhere else.

Laura, still in her stained pyjamas and still feeling her empty stomach, walked over small children on the carpet or eating dried glue off their palms to peruse the empty refrigerator for fantasies.

When some lady in a pantsuit came, Jessica panicked: $2500 per child, per day, was the penalty for not adhering to the Daycare and Nurseries Act. Jessica threw diapers at the woman as she walked away, clipboard in hand. The next day, Laura woke up to find her mother packing her stuffed animals into plastic bags.

"Come on. You're going to your dad's."

Ms Hina's hijab was not bejewelled like Mrs Kamal's. It was simple and dusty blue. Laura wondered if the pin near her right ear adhered the hijab to her head like a staple, but she didn't dare touch it.

"Did you want to help me make the snack?" Ms Hina asked after she saw that Cory was asleep on the couch. Another bender.

Laura watched with wonder at Ms Hina spreading cream cheese between two saltine crackers. Carefully and with graceful brown hands, she angled the sharp knife and peeled the apples. Peeled them the way Laura shaved her body in her mother's absence.

Ms Hina sat Laura down at the snack table and placed a coffee filter in front of her. She placed the crackers on it, along with cucumbers. Laura did not start eating voraciously, as she usually did. Instead, she sat with her hands in a fist on her lap.

"Did you have something to show me?" Laura nodded. She opened up her fists to show Ms Hina a weathered foam letter *u*. Laura had picked away at the foam while thinking of words to use. "Oh. My. You really thought about this, didn't you? What words did you discover?"

"Umbrella?" Laura was unsure.

"You're right! You got it, miss." Laura didn't want to tell her the other *u* words she learned: "unlucky" and "ugly."

"Are you ready for the next letter?" Ms Hina went to the cabinet. "This is the letter *g*. Guh–guh–gorilla. Can you promise me to find more words that start with this letter?" Laura nodded, then began eating.

MS HINA

O Canada! Our home and native land! ...

It was the last morning before Christmas holidays, and the kids stood like penguins listening to the national anthem. This was a particularly painful version of it. I hate Celine Dion. I hate her happy life. But really and truly, I hate her version of the anthem.

The kids seemed equally unimpressed. Toes rubbing against the insides of ankles. Toddlers wobbling under the weight of their huge heads. Noses picked. Heads scratched. I adjusted the pins on my hijab.

One more day before vacation.

"Are we going to sing some Christmas carols?" said Fern, a home daycare provider, while adjusting the Santa hat on her head. Since she was one of the very few moneyed folks at the centre, I always found her questions so off-putting. They were not so much questions as they were passive-aggressive, white lady demands. She briefly looked at my hijab and then flashed a tight-lipped smile.

"I have some songs planned," I replied, wanting to kick her and her Christian supremacist ass out of the centre.

I blew my wooden train whistle and announced to the children, "It's cleanup time! Everybody, clean up so we can have story time." I positioned myself beside three different toy boxes to help the kids with sorting.

"Bing? Are you cleaning up?" Of course he wasn't. He was still playing dress-up. Much to his chagrin, Edna pointed with her lips toward the hooks where the costumes belonged. He pouted and dragged his feet forward.

Sylvie pushed the broom across the floor to gather bits of play-dough before her brother Johnny could eat it. "Thank you, sweet Sylvie. I really appreciate your hard work," I told her. She smiled.

Laura silently approached me. Besides snack time, cleanup was her favourite. She seemed to enjoy one-on-one time with me to sort dollhouse furniture from train tracks. "Are you ready? Steady, Eddie." I said to her. She got to work, looking at each object and placing it in the correct box. When she completed her task, I gave Laura a high-five and caught her father looking at me disapprovingly, as per usual. He did not help with cleanup, nor did he supervise it. I was not surprised.

"Is everyone ready for circle time?" The kids moved like robots. They knew to come to the carpet and sit cross-legged. Since they were still, some of the caregivers took this opportunity to wipe snot off noses. One mother did a diaper change in the corner. Everyone winced as an invisible cloud of poop stink rose in the air.

I addressed my audience. "Can I see everyone's magic guitar?" I pulled from the sky my air guitar and pretended to strum. "You guys can choose what size guitar you want. Maybe you want a small one, like a ukulele, or you may want a big electric guitar. Your choice." The kids followed suit without question and positioned their arms around their imaginary instruments.

"I have a special friend named Micah, and he's an alien from outer space. He's green all over and because he isn't human, he eats things he's not supposed to. So, if you hear something that's gross, can I hear a yucky sound?"

"Eeeew!" "Yucky!" screamed the crowd of children.

"Perfect! Okay, here goes." I pretend strummed an introductory banjo riff, then sang.

> *Micah is my Martian friend.*
> *We're intergalactic pals until the end.*
> *He likes to eat dirty diapers!*

The kids screamed, smelling the actual diaper stink in the garbage can.

> *And he likes to eat boogers!*

A parent hooked her finger around the finger of a toddler digging into his own nostril. "No nose picking, please. No, thank you." I continued.

> *Micah is my Martian friend.*
> *We're intergalactic pals until the end.*
> *He likes to eat playdough!*
> *And he likes to eat pasta!*

I paused for effect.

> *With poop on top.*
> *Micah is my Martian friend!*

I held the note while working the neck of my air guitar, my tongue sticking out like I was a member of the band *Kiss*.

"Big finish, folks! Now, smash your guitar! Smash it!" We all pretended to smash our air guitars à la Jimi Hendrix. It was hilarious. I flashed a naughty smile at Fern in her Santa hat, still waiting for a Christmas carol.

By the end of the day, I was concerned some of the families who relied on the snacks in my program were going to be in need during the two-week hiatus. It wasn't my imagination that the program's grocery bill was climbing. I couldn't keep milk, cereal, or cheese in my pantry long enough. These kids were hungry. I wasn't sure if they had lunch, let alone dinner. So I served them snacks, willingly, plentifully, and without judgment.

I filled four different boxes with non-perishable items. Spaghetti noodles. Mushroom soup. Kraft Dinner. And I was able to up the grocery order, to ensure these usual food bank favourites were embellished with "leftovers" from the fridge: fresh milk, butter, bread, sweet potatoes, cucumbers, carrots, and cheese. I wanted to add more, perhaps a chicken or two, but I was sure management would catch on.

"I am not sure who wants to take these boxes home," I said as a general announcement to the literacy centre's regulars, knowing full well who was going to take them home. "But they are free for the taking." As predicted, Sylvie's family took a box. Anna, the woman who cares for three of her grandchildren while her daughter is in rehab, took one. Lady and her family took a box. She's the single mom just about to graduate from nursing school. Usually, it's her mother Pamela who comes in to take care of the kids, so seeing Lady was a pleasant surprise.

The fridge was empty. The toys were played with, then washed and put away.

Once it was quiet, I noticed Laura looking outside at the falling snow. Her hair was greasy as ever, thanks to the recurring lice; however, it was growing in nicely and tied together in a ponytail.

"Are you looking forward to your holidays?" I said to her. Laura nodded and pointed at the snow. "I know. It looks like we are going to get a big dump of snow." She smiled. Her eyes danced, like she remembered something. She reached into her pocket and showed me the foam letter *g* I had given her.

"You remembered! Did you come up with any words for me?"

She nodded. "Guh–guh–great. Guh–guh–goodbye." My stomach turned at that last word. To not see Laura for two weeks hurt my heart. I had grown so accustomed to seeing her and her sweet face at the centre.

I went to the cabinet to retrieve the other letters, then I placed them side by side on the windowsill. *H-U-G.* "Can you see what this spells? What sound does *h* make?"

"Huh–huh–huh." Laura held her hand in front of her mouth the way I had showed her, to feel the exhale of air.

I pointed to the *u.* "Uh–uh–uh." I nodded, smiled, then pointed to the *g.*

"Guh–guh–guh."

"So, let's stick these sounds together."

She obliged as my finger pointed to each letter. "Huh–uh–guh."

"Hug. Can you see? You read a word all by yourself. It says hug. Is it okay if I give you a hug?"

She smiled the biggest smile I ever saw her make. She reached out her arms. I held her. Her tiny body. My chin rested on her oily hair. She melted into me. I wanted to lift her up but thought better of it. I just was so happy. She let me hug her.

Her eyes met mine with a sudden look of fear. "Are you okay?"

The washroom adjacent to our room made a flushing sound, and out came Cory, adjusting his belt. He looked suspiciously between me and his daughter. "What are you doing to my daughter?"

I gulped. "Laura just spelled the word 'hug.' I'm so proud of her." Laura hung her head low.

"Laura Loo, come here right now." Laura did as she was told, and they began walking toward the door.

"Wait!" I called out to Cory. "Here. Did you want the last food box? It will go to waste otherwise."

He looked at the box on the windowsill. "I don't want your food box. I don't want you hugging my kid." He took Laura's hand and began walking out the door.

"No ... I don't think you understand. We had just spelled the word 'hug,' and I asked her to ..." There was no point. They were out the door. My face was hot with anger, with fear.

Cory glanced back at me, the usual look of disdain on his face. His lip twitched. I waited and hoped Laura would look back too, but Cory shut the door.

My body shuddered at its sound. I suddenly remembered being in grade five, watching a *National Geographic* film in class. The one with the gorilla mothering the kitten.

In that darkened classroom, I could feel my body releasing urine through my panties, through my Wrangler jeans, on to the plastic seat of my desk. I tried to sit on the heel of my running shoe to make it stop, but the flow was unstoppable. My pants, my shoe, the floor beneath me was soaked in urine. My swollen, inflamed belly informed the nurses that I needed an emergency appendectomy. Despite this being a medical emergency I couldn't help it, I was so ashamed to have peed my pants in front of my classmates. They thought it was so funny.

On the operating table, I felt the anesthetic drip into me, cold as ice up my arm, and I could feel myself peeing all over myself again as my eyes dimmed.

"Oh, shit!" I heard the surgeon say as I drifted off into dreamland. Even in an emergency, I couldn't do anything right.

There was something about the way Cory left that day with Laura. Something about it made me remember my subconscious understanding that I was being cut open. I was being dissected. Then I was being sewn up, with something missing inside. Something about that moment. It made me remember the scalpels. The bright lights. The blood.

I watched them leave, knowing I should say something. Anything. But all I did was rub my arms and belly, thinking of blood and knives all over me.

SYLVIE

It was Christmas Eve, and Mama happily prepared whatever we chose to eat from the box that Ms Hina had given us. Instant mashed potatoes. Duncan Hines devil's food cake. Eggs. We were full to the brim.

"Yes. For the millionth time, I will let you open your gifts tonight, but you have to sit the hell down and eat. You've got ants in your pants, Sylvie!"

All of the children had got together to decorate Michelle's office door. She pretended she was all surprised to see the construction paper disaster. She could barely find her doorknob.

"And who is this?" Michelle pointed at a Picasso version of herself, with shredded newspaper as her dreadlocks. All the kids giggled and rolled on the ground, unable to contain themselves. "Is this supposed to be me? Who made this? Who?" I raised my hand shyly, and we all laughed so hard.

Back in our room, Dad sat on the couch, relaxing after his meds, because the pain was for forever, Mama said. I propped him up with a pillow and played doctor with my new stethoscope.

"Breathe in," I said, while placing the contraption to his knee. "Breathe out."

I scribbled on a piece of wrapping paper, making extra sure not to make eye contact with my patient.

"It looks like you are going to be A-okay, Mr Beaudoin."

"Is that so?" Daddy said through his clenched jaw. It never closed the same after that accident.

"Yup. You just need your meds."

"That's what they all tell me." I wrapped Dad's head with my scarf, just like the bandage he had on after his accident.

"Pssst." Dad gestured for me to come closer and whispered in my ear. "When I get better, wanna come with me to the track again?" Woodbine Racetrack was the kind of place where parents looked through the windows at the action but not at their kids. I ran around, made forts out of restaurant tables, and played tag in the lobby with the other unsupervised children. That's what happens when you're born a kid and not a horse, I guess. Dad pretended he was helping Mama by taking me for the day. In truth, he was spending his time betting on slim chances. I knew his injuries would never get better, so when he asked me, I pretended too.

"Sure." I smiled at him.

Johnny hummed and tore wrapping paper for hours, until all that was left was a pile of moist pulp. Mama didn't mind. It kept him busy.

I played doctor with Daddy until his meds made him drift off to dreamland. After eating my fill of cake, I carefully crawled on to the side of his chest, careful not to knock out his tubes, and fell asleep. I could hear the sounds of his body working. The creaky floor sounds from his tummy. The swish of his blood. The pounding of his heart. It sounded like I was swimming and listening to the sounds of water beneath the surface of my father. This was my dad.

MICHELLE

There were a lot of hugs that Christmas Eve. I've been supervising the Galloway Shelter for seven years now. Each year, it's the time our residents find the hardest to endure. Lots of tears. Lots of calls to their families to say "hello," when really they want to say "I love you," and "I am very sorry for everything." Those cases are the most difficult to watch unfold. The ones who can't go to their families for the holiday season. It doesn't matter if you're Christian, Muslim, or atheist. It doesn't matter. It is a cold world out there, and it is also the coldest time of year. It feels so very good to walk into a house, one that is warm with so many bodies inside it. To hear people talking and forks clanging over fresh food, glasses clinking over a big table. All of that feels so good.

For whatever reason—and there are so many—these people don't have that choice. They're here in the shelter, and so am I. I always take this shift. Moving from suite to suite, I check in on everyone. Lots of hugs.

"I know, I know. I hear everything you're saying, and that is damn hard."

"Hey, look at me. You are going to take this one breath at a time. Soon you'll be lying down, wondering how you'll get through the night, but you will. You will. And tomorrow is a new day."

That night, I came to my office and saw what I expected. The kids went and decorated my door. I am always amazed that these families will go through the trouble of going to the dollar store to buy trinkets of all kinds to tape to my door. I could barely find the knob. I have to tell you, even though this happens every single year, I still get misty-eyed. The kids think it's so funny, especially when I pretend to be surprised.

That Native kid, Sylvie, proudly showed me the paper doll she made of me. She had taped it to the door herself. She made my face out of a brown paper bag to match my skin. My dreadlocks were made out of strips from the *Toronto Star* newspaper. The entire real estate section was used to illustrate my hair. Poor thing must have used up all her tape.

"How's your dad?" I asked her.

"Asleep on the couch."

Sylvie's dad was on that couch for months. Jonathon, like many here, was a sad combination of bad cards dealt and bad choices made.

Later that night, I headed outside to have a cigarette. The air was crisp and clean and quiet. Nice change from the shelter. A lone car slowly drove past, leaving tracks behind it. I could tell by its fishtailing that the driver couldn't afford winter tires. I whispered a prayer to myself that there would be no accidents tonight.

"Faggot!" I squinted through the dark down Kingston Road toward the yelling. It was two men near that Everyting Taste Good Caribbean restaurant. One guy slipped on the ice while the other guy got in a car and drove off in a hurry. Now I realized the man was stumbling toward the shelter. Toward me.

As the crunch of snow got closer, I retreated into the shadows of our entrance. Judging by that eagle patch he had on his jacket, I knew to avoid men like him. He had an unlit cigarette in his mouth.

I put my cigarette out immediately. I didn't want him asking me for a light. I hoped he hadn't seen me. He was drunk, for sure. Even though the air was still, he wavered like a flame in the wind.

Suddenly the entrance door flew open, and my head snapped to the side. Christy. As per usual, she was engrossed in her boyfriend drama. When she saw me, she ended her phone call and gave me a weak wave.

"Hi, Michelle. Can I ask you something?" Christy didn't wait for me to answer. "Is the Number 86 bus running tonight? I just need to head out, you know?" She checked her phone for new texts.

I have seen so many like Christy come and go here at the shelter. They come when they're young. They come when they've been touched by their fathers, their cousins, their brothers. They come when their social worker has a binder full of notes under their arm. They come with their plastic bags and dollar store purses over their bony shoulders. They come with dreams, big and small, wanting to be my next success story. They come wanting love, and so they hug me long before night falls, because in another world it would have been their mother kissing them goodnight and not their uncle kissing them on the couch. They come. They come when they are old. They come with babies sucking their soft and saggy breasts. They come with children, all looking like their different daddies, licking lollipops and wearing old Halloween costumes.

Just yesterday, I watched a woman collapse on the tile of the front foyer. She watched as her kids were taken away by her auntie, who happened to be the only sober one in the immediate family. I watch people choose lovers and drugs over kids all the time.

As I was about to answer Christy and let her know the 86 bus was out of commission until nine o'clock tomorrow morning, she jolted from the vibration of another text coming in. It was him. Finally. She waved again at me and headed back inside.

When am I going to see Christy again? I wondered to myself.

I looked back in the direction of the drunk white man, but he was gone.

CINDY

Eunice was such a pro that night. All I had to do was put the Christmas wrapper from the kids' presents down on the ground, and she knew what she needed to do. I saw it in her face. Like, her tear ducts get all weepy. Her teats get all full, ready for her pups. I could see it from the dinner table, where I was sitting. I knew we were going to have Christmas puppies. She has had about five litters with me. All of those puppies sold like hotcakes. But puppies born on Christmas? What a score.

So, anyway. I gathered all the wrapping paper from the kids' presents and made a manger just like Jesus had. Except I was the only one there for the Nativity. No wise men. No kings. No bloody Mary and Joseph. Just me, Cindy Brown, in my Walmart holiday pyjamas. In the kitchen. It was a hoot.

I knew I might be there a while, considering how old Eunice is. So I double-layered cushions and put three kitchen chairs together to lie down on in case I got sleepy.

Before I sat my ass down, I slid the lace curtains of my kitchen window to the side to see if anyone in our community housing cul-de-sac was making the move to do Christmas fireworks like last year. There was no one but that Black boy, Victor, walking to his house. I could see him looking back behind him, like he was suspicious of someone following him. Wouldn't put it past him to do something stupid on Christmas. I don't expect much of him, after his arrest. I heard he was vandalizing with his paints. What a shame. Victor waved at me, and my face got hot. Quickly, I slid the curtain closed.

"Mom?" Travis came in, looking all sleepy. I fingered his haircut. God almighty. I must've given him the worst haircut on the surface of this planet. I was being stupid, watching HGTV while cutting my kid's hair. I couldn't help it. I love watching home improvement shows. You know how you can't watch naked body porn in the presence of your kids. But you can watch house porn, get all turned on by the prospect of crown moulding and double vanities while you eat dinner with your ungrateful family. Only problem is, it makes me the worst hairdresser. Not like I need any help with that.

"Are they here yet?" Travis had seen so many puppies being born. Before Eunice, it was Wendy, a Shih Tzu. They were named after my mother's ugly sisters.

I still have pictures of Travis and Gabby dressing up Wendy's puppies in baby clothes, standing on carpet covered in dog turds. It was sad as hell when Wendy started barfing uncontrollably, morning and night. I had to shell out cash just to have the vet look at her. He said, all judgmental-like, "How many litters has she had?" As if he couldn't tell I was in the business of selling puppies. I know it was him who called the cops on us. I could smell his suspicion. By the time they busted open my garage door and found Wendy in her cage, fooling them with her pretend shakes—she always did that to get pity from anyone she met, what a drama queen!—we had done one of those midnight move-outs to avoid the damage fees from our landlord. I knew that asshole would be coming at us, wondering about the pile of dog shit on the balcony. I was doing her a favour anyway, what with all the barking and such. I still miss Wendy, though.

"Not yet, mister." Travis sat on my lap and put his head into my neck. Of all my four kids, it took the longest to get him off the boob. Lord, what a little perv.

I could tell by the way his breath smelled that he hadn't brushed his teeth like I'd told him to. This is what happens when you send him to school with a bunch of Caribbean people. Like, they have no manners, you know? One friend of mine who is ashamed of his Guyanese roots told me that when he was growing up, his family would have a sink full of dirty dishes and would clean them only when they needed them. Thankfully, he married some Chinese woman who wouldn't take that crap. I mean, who grows up like that? People don't get what it's like to be one of only a few white kids in a bad school.

Back when I was attending grade school at St. Malachy, we were a small trashy lot. It was a cash-poor school, like, I am talking only one snare drum and one recorder in the school band kind of poor. Most of us were the grandchildren of senior citizens who turned their cottages into their retirement homes. All of us smoking cigarettes at the back of the school, while our teachers thought we were in the gym for Easter mass. One day when we were punching holes in the bottoms of beer cans and sucking them dry, I saw a bus roll into the school driveway. It was full of people from El Salvador. All of them were refugees from the war down there. Suddenly our school was majority brown and majority English as a Second Language bullshit. Scarborough was never the same after that bus rolled in. Next came the Sri Lankans and all the other Pakis. The Chinese were sneaky; they were trickling in all along. Those Filipinos just kept having babies. Now I can't walk into Scarborough Town Centre without the lot of them taking up all the space in the food court, smelling like curry.

Travis smelled sour, which wasn't much better.

"I said to brush your teeth." He groaned like he always does. Like he was surprised he had to brush his teeth, yet again.

"But I wanna see the puppies being born."

"Okay, fine. Go brush your teeth for two whole minutes, and you can come watch and wait. I'll set the timer on the stove. Now go."

I couldn't blame him. It was exciting.

I remember when we all visited Riverdale Farm downtown. We took two trains and a streetcar to get there. I was in charge of two refugees from El Salvador. Both girls were dressed like Michael Jackson, trying to be hip, but with clothes from the Goodwill. It was so hard not to laugh. We were led to a barn door. Inside was this sow lying on her side, in so much pain. Poor thing looked right up at me. I could see her piglets all wiggling about in her belly. It was so crowded in that belly, I could see their snouts and tails. The skin was so taut. I approached her with caution, wondering if she would bite me. I rubbed her head. She closed her eyes. I could see it felt good.

I did the same to Eunice that night. I do the same to any dog about to give birth. I rubbed her head. She closed her eyes because it felt good. There was something about these puppies that was different, you know? Like something in my tummy told me things were going to change.

WINSUM

All you gotta do is take off your apron, put on a nice dress, and sit at the table in front of the counter instead of behind it. And ta-dah! All of a sudden, you're at a restaurant that doesn't belong to you. No explaining to white people how spicy this is or how spicy that is. No checking the expiry date on bottles of Ting or wiping down the tops of Chubby pop drinks. No dealing with malfunctioning freezers. The only task I had was to wipe away enough frost on the restaurant window so the "closed" sign could be seen, loud and proud for the holidays.

For Christmas Eve, I had sent Melvin into the kitchen to do as I said. To let me put my feet up a bit. Christmas Eve was for me and my family. I had hired Melvin to help out at my restaurant after my sister begged me. Little Caesars had fired him for making "culinary choices" to people's pizzas without their consent. Because he fancies himself a chef extraordinaire, he thought it was a good idea to add random toppings like sundried tomatoes and capers to a basic cheese pizza order.

While my foolish nephew took over the kitchen, me and my new wig were up front and centre, thank you very much. I had given Melvin strict instructions to simply plate my usual turkey, macaroni pie, some pastelles, and chow chow for dinner. But even with that, he was banging away in the kitchen. I shook my head.

Lorna sat across from me, chatting away. Clive sat beside his wife, reading the latest issue of *Sharenews*.

"There is something so very precious about Switzerland, you know?"

"No, I do not." I admired my fresh tips that I got at the nail salon down the road.

"Winsum, it is a magical, glorious place. Our Airbnb was in Valais. Right, Clive?"

Clive nodded silently and turned the page of the newspaper.

"Or was it La Sage? Well, it doesn't matter. The point is, we were surrounded by the Swiss Alps. It was like we were in a movie."

Lord, have mercy on my sad soul, but truly I hate listening to her brag. I know Christ has my back and understands the hours I have spent as a single mom working my behind off for my restaurant and putting my son Joffrey through nursing school. Listening to this woman go off about skiing here and there has earned me a cent or two in the heaven bank!

"You don't say."

"Absolutely. We had a chalet at the bottom of the hill so that Melvin could snowboard right down to us and then eat lunch."

Clive kept reading.

"Doesn't it seem silly?" I asked Lorna. "Sliding down a hill of snow and paying money for it. Wouldn't you rather visit our cousins in Port of Spain?"

"It's not all about sand and sun, Winsum. You travel for culture. The Europeans have culture. Did you know the Swiss can speak German, French, and Italian?"

"So what of it? Our family speaks Spanish and English. On top of that, Mom spoke Cantonese."

"It's not the same." She rolled her eyes and changed the subject. "It's too bad Joffrey couldn't make it."

"Well, you know *my* son." I made sure to put emphasis on mine, as opposed to her sad specimen of a child. "I wish Joffrey could make his way down to Toronto, but he's too busy working at Channaman's Island Restaurant, in Montreal, while he's finishing school. My boy is a good apple."

"It's so funny, you know? When you told me he was studying to be a nurse, I thought you were joking. I didn't even know boys could be nurses."

I wanted to rip the cheap wig off her head.

"Dinner is served!"

Melvin plunked down a square plate in front of mc. Where the hell did he get square plates? Did he steal them from the Keg? On these stupid square plates sat a palmful of delicately handcrafted fanciness stuffed into square pasta shells and drizzled with the most pretentious zigzag of pepper sauce. Curried chickpeas dotted the edges of each plate like rabbit turds.

"Trinidadian Doubles ... but ravioli!" His arm flourished in a rainbow arc a wee bit too close to my new wig.

"What in God's name—"

"Trinidadian Doubles—" his arm flourished again, but I stopped it mid-arc, to get it away from my beautiful wig.

"No, I heard you. What in God's name do you think you're doing?"

"It's Doubles ... but in a ravioli instead of in a *bara*."

I crossed my arms and stood to meet his clueless gaze.

"What next? You gonna make Jamaican coco bread croissants?!"

I could see in his face that the wheels were turning over a good idea. I stomped my foot down as hard as the tiles could take.

Knowing full well the idiocy of his own son but not possessing the balls to do anything about it, Clive folded his paper in half, placed it under his arm, and began shuffling out. I always knew him to be soft, a bit cowardly. If I dug really deep into that yellow heart of his, I know he would have a few words to say about his sorry excuse of a wife and son. Instead, he silently put his brown leather jacket on. He neatly tucked his striped scarf into the edges of his collar to guard against the cold and our bickering.

"Look. Now my Clive is all vexed. He's leaving. See what you're doing? It's Christmas Eve, and you're here barking orders left, right, and centre."

"You listen here. This is my restaurant. I told you, no silly business up in my kitchen. We were going to have a simple family dinner of turkey, chow chow, macaroni pie, and pastelles. That's all."

Clive spirited away, out of the restaurant. A grandfather heron flying into the darkness of a marsh. We were more like turkeys, my sister being longer in the neck and with much less sense than feathers.

"Winsum, this is what you serve every day at Everyting Taste Good. Maybe Melvin just wanted to spice things up or something."

"Lorna, this is tradition. Tell me something now. What was the name of Mom's restaurant right beside Warden Station?"

"Everyting Taste Good."

"And how many years was Everyting Taste Good the number

one place to get the best Doubles in Scarborough?"

"Fifteen years," Lorna looked down at her hands, "until Mom died."

"That's right. And every Christmas, we would go close down the shop and have the restaurant to ourselves. Every Christmas. Until Mom died. That's why I opened this joint. To continue her traditions. And now, Everyting Taste Good has been here for eight years and is the number-one island restaurant in Scarborough."

I turned to Melvin once again.

"People here want home. They want home because it is so darn cold outside, and all they want is their mom or dad or kids back where it's warm. And green. They want it how it is back home. Looks ugly and tastes pretty. Simple. Served with a big spoon on a big plate. No fuss. No thinking about texture and height and taste journey or whatever. They just want home. Today is Christmas dinner. I want home. None of this foolishness. Now, go back to the kitchen and serve me home. Now."

Melvin turned on his heels and slowly walked back to the kitchen. His ball cap rim snapped back in my direction to make one last, insulting plea.

"But, Auntie—"

"Don't 'but Auntie' me. Go in there and learn the beauty of big spoons and big plates."

CLIVE

When the door shut behind me, I was greeted by the quiet of a winter night. Silent night. Fit for a king. Fit for Baby Jesus.

I checked my watch. Five thirty. I had been in there for only an hour. It felt like an eternity. I had very little time. I would be expected to return before Winsum served her Black Cake for dessert. Perhaps by then their battle would have died down to a peaceful stalemate, I reasoned.

I smelled the booze before I heard his voice.

"Hey." I turned to see a filthy white man pointing weakly at the restaurant's frosted windows.

"Good evening."

"This is the place with the free chicken, right?"

"Excuse me?"

"We got the free chicken. Last time. We had so much free chicken."

Maybe he was referring to when Winsum's refrigerator broke down. "Oh, right. There's no free chicken tonight. It's closed."

"It's not closed." He staggered toward the window and with his red cold hands tried to wipe the frost off to look inside. "I can see people in there."

I blocked him gently with my arm, not wanting a fight or a scene. "Yes, but they're eating alone in there. It's not open to the public right now, sir."

"Listen, can you ask them if there's free chicken like last time?"

He used his fingers to twist his lips, searching for the words so hard that he almost ripped them off. His voice cracked as he looked at his soaking wet sneakers. "Listen, man. I forgot. I woke up and forgot the stores would be closed. And my daughter ... she's up there in my apartment, and now we have no dinner. I forgot it was ... I just forgot. I slept too long."

"This place is open, though." I pointed to Mr Park's convenience store right next door.

"I just came from there. The chink thought I was stealing." His sobs were so absurd, I wasn't sure if he was crying or laughing. I was too embarrassed to look him in the eye.

"I can hear everyone else down the hall having parties and laughing. And she's hungry ... I don't know if I can do this, man."

There was a heaviness in my heart. I reached into my pocket but only found a toonie.

"Here. I'm sorry, that's all I have."

"What the hell can I buy with that?"

"I don't know. Maybe some bread? I don't know."

"I just need you to go in there and ask for the fucking free chicken. I don't want bread, man."

I put the toonie back into my pocket. He was getting much too confusing. "Please, go home. The restaurant is closed. I'm sorry." I reached out again and gently tried to steer him away from the door. He whipped my hand off his bomber jacket.

"Get your hands off me." I raised my hands up. I didn't want a fight. "You think I want your fucking chicken? It's probably rotten. That's why it's closed. Nobody wants your fucking chicken." He tried to compose himself but slipped on the ice. I reached out to steady him.

"Don't touch me, you fucking faggot." I froze. My jaw tightened. "I can see it all over your face. Get off me. Don't touch me." He slipped again. I wanted so badly to kick his teeth in, he was so close to my shoe.

Instead, I said, "You're a disgrace." A fog lingered around my mouth after I said the words. "Your daughter deserves better. You are a disgrace as a father. Go home and change things. Or let her be fathered by someone else."

I left him lying on the ice, dumbfounded. I opened my car door, got in, and slammed it shut. I waited until he got up. He looked at me in way I wasn't sure if he was rolling his eyes or trying to steady his drunken gaze, then stumbled across the street, a clumsy silhouette passing between street lamps. When he was out of my vision, my throat let out one sharp sob. I stifled it. I knew I wasn't speaking just to him but to the ghosts of my past.

I started the car and headed to Manse Road. Over train tracks and black ice, over snow mounds and ditches, to my special place. There was no time to peruse Craigslist casual encounters. I drove, despite having no snow tires, just for the slight chance that maybe East Point Bird Sanctuary would be happening.

The gates to the sanctuary were rusted brown, framing an expanse of dark forest. The sky that hung over this clandestine meeting place glowed pink, like a beacon to all who gathered. I parked the Corolla haphazardly near a snowbank, half burying my weathered all-season tires. If I had to dig them out with my bare hands, I didn't mind. I just had to go into the deep and dark.

Realizing I was dressed for a holiday dinner and not for a romp in the snow, I opened the trunk to find my rubber shoe covers. Standing on one leg at a time, I managed to slip them over my leather loafers. I thumbed the bulge of condoms in the pocket of my trousers and adjusted my erection with the other hand. I marched through the snow, the crunch-crunch-crunch of the snow, to my truth.

Like magic, through the thick bush a landscape of bodies emerged before my eyes. The last of this year's leaves applauded the debauchery below as the wind ripped through the branches. What first looked like a few turned into many as they writhed, keeping rhythm with each other, making music of their sinfulness.

I was surprised. I had been worried it would be slim pickings tonight, considering it was Christmas Eve. I was wrong.

"Excuse me," a young blond man who appeared from the bushes said. The bottom of his T-shirt was lifted up and tucked behind his head, revealing a six-pack and newly pink skin. He was putting himself together as he rushed past me. Steam rose from his body. Soon that would be me, I thought.

I walked farther toward the dramatic waves of Lake Ontario and found a clearing. Here, there was more pink sky than forest. A couple of silhouettes stood in the clearing, kissing deeply. I was frozen in my wanting. My cheeks grew warm in the cold night air, watching the couple swallow each other up. They caught their breaths for a moment, their foreheads touching. They seemed to have just come up to the water's surface, they were breathing so hard. Then they realized I, too, was breathing hard with them.

I approached with trepidation. They stood looking at me, undecided, then offered a gesture of welcome.

When kisses keep lips warm, when bodies merge to keep frostbite at bay, it's exhilarating. This was our game. This romp under the pink sky of winter was survival. Skin bitten by chattering teeth. Cold dicks sucked inside the oven of mouths. Pants lowered and held tightly between calf muscles to keep them dry so that we could return to our wives with the guise of having gotten some fresh air. When, in truth, we were on a cliff overlooking the lake, bent in half over a rock, feeling the power of a complete stranger.

We were the men who knew the power of blending in at cocktail parties, who kept our opinions neutral around the water cooler, who knew to nod in recognition at our wives' stories.

"Wasn't Hilda's garden an eyesore?" they might ask.

"Yes, dear," we would answer absentmindedly while checking Craigslist postings on our phones.

We perfected the art of shuddering in disgust when told the new neighbour down the street was a proud homosexual, and we perfected the art of cumming in that proud homosexual's mouth that evening in a park at a circle jerk coordinated amongst us. We held our newspapers up high, and we kept our activities on the down-low.

But here. Here, we were naked from the calves up, thrusting our truths into the assholes of strangers. Here, I was thrusting my sorrow into the blackness of night, a memory of a disgraceful father.

When we were done, we zipped our trousers back into place and headed back to our cars. I felt like howling at the moon. I always do.

I returned to Everyting Taste Good, to my family silently eating Black Cake. I helped myself to a slice, without pomp and circumstance. From where I sat, I could see the handprint of that filthy man on the restaurant's window.

CLARA

"Clara, stop staring out the window," Daddy said.

"Then why leave the curtains open all the time?" I asked before taking a step back.

"Well, that's so that everyone else can look in," he said. "It's good for the neighbourhood to see what a proper house looks like."

Even from this far away, I could continue spying on that island restaurant. Through the alleyway, between two sets of townhomes across the street from us, I could see a family sitting there eating. It was Christmas Eve.

"Clara Jane Donohue ..." The way Daddy said it, I knew he meant business. I turned on the heels of my patent leather Christmas shoes toward my father, who sat at the head of our long wooden table, his middle finger swiping pages across his tablet. He didn't even need to look at me. "Get away from the window or I will tell Santa to skip our house."

I played along. He didn't know that my classmate Hakim had already told me Santa wasn't real. At first, I thought he was just saying that because he is Muslim. But then Sylvie and Bing told me Santa was a lie too.

Sylvie had told me one day after we played tag, "My mama said she couldn't afford two gifts for Christmas, so she had to spill the beans. Plus, Mama says she's tired of old white men taking the credit for things." My eyes started getting all watery. I didn't want to say goodbye to all those presents.

I remember coming home that day and thinking about this for a long while. I sat at the top of the stairs watching my parents argue about how to put our holiday stockings on top of the gas fireplace without drilling holes into the rock surface.

"Who the hell designs a fireplace with no mantel, Edward? Who?! What is a fireplace good for, if you can't put stockings or family photos on it?"

"Someone who would rather watch this high-definition television!"

"You're full of shit!"

"You're full of doughnuts!"

My mom covered her lower belly with her sweater, embarrassed.

I didn't want to cause any more trouble by bringing up the Santa lie. If I kept pretending I didn't know, I could continue getting extra gifts. And, really, Santa was just some old white man. My dad was close enough. Why make them even more upset?

So, on Christmas Eve I played along and asked Daddy if I could see the app on his phone again. He sighed and pulled it out. It was a graphic of radar straddling a map of the world. On this map, a blinking light with a ping sound was supposed to be radar picking up the signal of Santa and his sleigh travelling the world, giving gifts.

"There's Santa!" I pointed eagerly on the screen. Daddy brushed my oily finger away, then wiped the surface of his beloved phone on his reindeer sweater.

"That's right, Princess."

I noticed the blinking light on the screen took its time over Europe, but when it moved over the continent of Africa, it zipped through.

"Why did it just rush through Africa?" I asked.

"That's because little children in Africa are perfectly fine with sticks."

That explained it.

Dinner was served, and my job was to wake Uncle Olly, who fell asleep looking for something to watch on Netflix. His legs were sprawled, and his mouth was wide open. I tried to close his mouth, and it shocked him into sitting up. As he rocked his body to a standing position, he asked me, "So, Clara, did you make cookies for Santa to eat?"

I showed him a plate of chocolate chip cookies I made with Mom earlier that afternoon.

Uncle Olly looked around, confused. "Where is Jason? Isn't he coming down for dinner too?"

My mom, whose back was to us while she carved the turkey, suddenly went still. She took a breath and kept carving. Jason was away, at least for now. He would be back. Not sure when, but some time, some day.

Daddy opened the liquor cabinet looking for the bottles Mom and he had saved for the holidays. Some red wine they picked up on their last trip to Niagara. It reminded him of good times. He proceeded to pour into everyone's glass except mine, with a little extra for himself. He thought I didn't see him place the remains of the bottle at the foot of his chair, but I did.

Mom kept going back and forth from the kitchen. She wasn't as smooth as she usually was for family dinners. Back and forth she went, to bring something she had forgotten. Napkins. The gravy boat. The gravy boat with gravy in it. Her juice concoction, since she was off alcohol for her cleanse.

I was already busy using my own fork to scoop pieces of turkey, stuffing, mashed potatoes, and all the other fixings onto my plate. My daddy slapped my wrist.

"For heaven's sakes, Clara. Show some decorum. Get serving spoons from the kitchen. Ask your mother where they are."

By the time we all sat down, my mom was handing out Christmas crackers of all different colours. Holding them between each other's hands, we looked like paper dolls.

My mom got serious. "Now that we are all holding hands—"

"We're not holding hands, Wendy. We're holding Christmas crackers. What is it now?"

"Edward. Will you please just let me finish?!" Mom took a breath. "I just thought that instead of doing grace before meals—"

"We're not religious, Wendy."

"I know that, Edward. There's a difference between being spiritual and being religious, all right? I just thought it would be nice to each take a turn saying what we are thankful for and what we wish for in the future."

Everyone struggled to keep our crackers up with our arms.

"Well, okay, I am thankful for this amazing food, and I wish we could eat it. Now, how is that?"

"Thank you, Edward, for your brief and succinct participation. Okay, my turn. I am so very thankful that Uncle Olly has driven all the way from Bancroft to be here."

Uncle Olly turned to me and whispered in my ear, "So, Clara, did you make cookies for Santa to eat?"

My mom continued, "I am thankful for having shelter in our lives, safety, my beautiful daughter, and—"

"And Jason!" Uncle Olly added with a giggle, looking to his left and realizing there was an empty spot beside him. That very empty seat still had that worn armrest; the armrest Jason picked at waiting for dinner to be over so he could go out, to where only he knew.

"And Jason."

My dad shifted in his seat. He took a sip from his wine glass. He looked down at his ankle where he had placed the remaining wine.

"And I wish for world peace, for the environment to be healed, for a mild winter. Yes, that's it."

I knew that wasn't it. She wished Jason would come home.

We finally pulled hard on the crackers. Loud snaps were heard, and we all let out a weak "yaaaaaay." Inside my cracker was a paper crown, which I placed on my head. The string on the little plastic yo-yo inside was too tangled to actually play with.

Both my parents and I ate quietly while Uncle Olly started with his long stories.

"Back when I was a child, we were never allowed to open our presents until we all heard the Queen's speech on the CBC Radio."

Uncle Olly continued, surprised no one was interrupting him.

"We would just sit there in our pyjamas, looking at our gifts and listening to her talk all proper on the radio. I don't understand some-times why we do the things we do. The Queen never knew us. She said things that didn't make sense. I never understood a word she said. I just wanted my presents. If Santa was on the radio, I would listen all day. But the Queen is just some old lady in England with fancy clothes and a fancy house, you know?"

That night, after everyone was supposed to be asleep, I sat at the top of the stairs and watched my parents listen to a voicemail message that Jason left for them that evening. The one time my dad left his phone somewhere else instead of in his pants pocket, and Jason called. They played it again and again. My mother fell into Daddy's arms, crying. They agreed to save the message.

"Sounds like he's homesick."

Daddy kissed my mom on her forehead, then patted her stiffly three times on the back. It was game time.

My mom took the plate of chocolate chip cookies and ate half of one. Using her left hand, she messily wrote on a note, "Thanks for the cookies. Love Santa."

My daddy went outside. Before he left tracks in the snow with a baseball bat to look like reindeer hooves, he pulled a funny looking cigarette out of his pocket—the same funny cigarette he pulls out each time he and Mom have an argument—and smoked it on our porch. When he returned inside, he ate the rest of the cookies on my Santa plate and licked the crumbs clean.

I went back to my bed sleepy and more excited than ever, believing that seeing Santa would not have been as miraculous as watching my parents work together to make me believe in him without arguing once.

BING

It was midnight mass at St. Malachy's Catholic Church on Morning-side Avenue. All the cool kids were asleep, waiting for Santa, while my mother and I, as well as what seemed to be the last of the devout Catholic Filipino population of Scarborough, were waiting for the return of Jesus.

All of us, and I mean all of us, reeked of pork. Crispy *pata*. *Giniling*. *Nilaga*. *Embutido*. You could smell it on our coats, on our breath; it wafted into the air when we made the sign of the cross; it spread like wildfire as we shook each other's hands. Like Jesus was not a sacrificial lamb, but rather, a sacrificial pig.

The only ones who smelled like chicken were the three Menendez sisters who owned the Happy Chicken on Morningside Avenue. Legend has it that Ate Lin, the eldest of the sisters, volunteered for many years to give personal support to a fellow parishioner—some old man knocking on death's door—including walking him to and from church. Just before the man kicked the bucket, he handed Ate Lin the keys to the Happy Chicken franchise, for *free*. This happened just weeks before the three sisters were finished their twenty-four months of service under the Live-In Caregiver Program, wiping baby bums and taking lip from abusive employers. What the legend does not account for is that Ate Lin's unclocked hours helping the old man in and out of his wheelchair and cooking his favourite adobo would have earned her a sizable portion of such a franchise, had she been paid fairly. Ma always said that food tasted better when it was free. And here, these ladies were making the sweetest-tasting fried chicken this side of Kingston Road.

I shook their hands and wished them a Merry Christmas. They pinched my cheeks, smoothed my hair, and asked about my girlfriend as a joke.

"Hoy. Bing. Look at how big you are now. Wow, *naman*. How is school?" they said with "Row Your Boat"-like phrasing. One of them, my Ate Lou, had braces, so she said the same thing but with a lateral lisp.

"Okay, *lang*, Ate," I said shyly while looking at my shiny black shoes. At the door of the church sat my winter boots, which I would change into once we were to head back outside.

I wanted to tell my Ates so badly that I had been kissed by the handsomest boy in school and that I wasn't sure where it was going to lead, but fingers crossed, we would venture to the nearest Dairy Queen together some time soon. But in real life, I knew it would halt their usual giggles and playing with my hair. Instead, I continued to look at the mirror of my shiny shoes.

"How is your mom?" Ma asked Ate Lin in a whisper as we entered the church. She dipped her middle finger into the holy water and made the sign of the cross lightly on herself so as not to ruin her makeup. We made our way to our pews. *El nombre del Padre, del Hijo y del Espíritu Santo*, Amen.

"Hallelujah, hallelujah, hallelujah," proudly sang a little boy from the downstage corner of the choir. Small in stature at only three feet, the hem of his white gown grazed the floor, and his songbook needed two hands to support. This call and response always sounds best with the highest, sweetest, most angelic voice.

A shuffling of bodies, the sound of creaking wood as the congregation stood and sang in response, "Hallelujah, hallelujah, hallelujah." The organ blared everyone awake once again after a sequence of sitting on hard, unforgiving pews and kneeling on squishy, unforgiving kneelers, hoping to be forgiven.

Father Joseph held the Eucharist high for everyone to see. I was looking forward to communion since I was so very hungry. I love the popcorn flavour in my mouth, as well as the chance to line up for it so I can show off my outfit. While the priest held the unleavened bread, I saw the flames of the Advent candles—now all four of them lit—waver. The flames grew tall, then moved side to side so brilliantly, I thought for a second they would set the pinecone wreath surrounding them on fire.

We shuffled like penguins to the side, past winter coats, past children who did not yet observe communion, to join the line of people ready to break bread with Christ.

While I was in line, a small blonde girl rushed past me and brushed against the sleeve of my dress shirt. She was so forceful, for a second I thought the button on my cuff was pulled off. She giggled.

"Laura?" I called out softly. What was she doing here?

Ma quickly adjusted my shoulders forward and said, "Shh." I looked up at her and saw that she was looking at the altar and not at the girl who had whizzed past. Had she not seen?

I tried to see where Laura had gone. I was concerned that she was in only a summer dress and not proper church clothes, especially because of the cold. But she was nowhere to be seen. There were so many people shuffling about, lining up for communion. They all towered over me while I peered between them trying to figure out where Laura went.

"Sssssst. Look forward." Ma gently adjusted me again in the line, as the priest approached.

We left the church close to one o'clock in the morning. We stood at the door taking turns changing our shiny shoes for our salt-stained winter boots. Carefully, in slow motion, and with a lot of giggles, Ma and I made our way back to our apartment building on Lawrence Avenue. Sheets of ice lay before us, each one a challenge. Ma held my hand as I skittered across an icy puddle, the threat of bubbles and water underneath its semi-frozen surface. I made it to the other side, leaving only a crack, like on the windshield of a car after an accident.

We heard a fire truck in the distance. My mother made the sign of the cross, as she usually does whenever an ambulance or a fire truck passes. *El nombre del Padre, del Hijo y del Espíritu Santo,* Amen. The sound of the truck came closer.

When it passed us and beat us to our own apartment building, my mother fell on a patch of ice. I helped her up. We rushed as fast as we could, suddenly impervious to the slip and fall, toward our home.

VICTOR

If you were to ask me for the exact details of the first time I was told cops are not to be trusted, to be truthful, I wouldn't even remember. It's like having a memory of when you first tie a shoe by yourself. The event was so long ago. And I was told by so many, and *trained* by so many to protect myself, that the act of stiffening in the presence of hatred toward Black men became, and still is, as routine as putting on a shoe. Rabbit ears through the loop. Pull the laces.

So when the cops began searching my red wagon full of paint for the bridge mural project, those boys barely had to tell me what to do. I could have done it myself.

I listen in on white people talking in office spaces or in food courts over lunch, about being pulled over for speeding or for other minor offences. They can laugh about it as something brief and bothersome. Sometimes shocking. They brag about the words or expressions that helped them weasel their way out. Perhaps they cried in front of them. Perhaps they pointed to their sleeping child in the backseat. Brief and bothersome.

That night with the paint, I saw the cops drive into the townhouse complex, and the hairs on my neck stood on end. I could see an ambulance, so I knew the cops weren't there for me. But I knew things could change. If you were to ask me exactly where I feel things when a cop is around, I would tell you I feel it between my ears, on the flat of my chest, the centre of my palms, and on the back of my tongue. Between my ears because I am thinking, *stay calm*. On the flat of my chest because I'm reminding myself to breathe. The centre of my palms because, in truth, I really wish I could slap somebody each time I'm stopped by a cop. And on the back of my tongue because I'm trying to strategize what to say when they ask me what I am doing.

"What are you up to?" one cop looked right at me and nodded toward the wagon. Another cop approached. He began poking around the bottles of paint. There were about eight bottles of acrylics, which were paid for by my grant.

"Where did you get this paint? They look pretty new."

"They are new, sir."

"You didn't answer my question. Where did you get them?"

"From Home Depot, sir."

"You bought paint from Home Depot."

"Yes, sir. I took the bus to the Morningside location. I purchased the paint myself."

"You did."

"Yes, sir."

"You bought this yourself? This new paint?"

"Yes, sir."

The centre of my palms were buzzing. Right below my eyes, heat was gathering, and my face was sweating.

"And why do you have this paint? You're painting some graffiti or something?"

"No, sir. I am an artist." Before I could even show them my sketchbook, one cop was prying open the bottles and leaving the caps off.

"It's green." To this day, I replay that cop saying that exact thing over and over in my head. "It's green." He said it officially, like it confirmed in his mind that I was up to no good. He even nodded at the other one who was standing close to my chest and breathing on my face.

"Please, don't open my paint. Please."

"Why can't we open them? If they're just paint, then there's nothing to hide."

"I'm asking you not to open them because they are paint, sir. I don't want them to dry out."

"I'm going to ask you step back."

"I haven't moved, sir."

"Step back."

"But I haven't moved, sir."

"Don't raise your voice at me."

The next thing I knew, I was taken to the station. I wasn't cuffed. But I was brought in. I sat in an office chair for five hours. No one would speak to me. And when I was let go, I realized I had just been given a police-sized version of time-out in the corner. It was so humiliating being driven in a cop car. Everyone in the housing complex looked at me like I was yet another Black boy doing no good. All of these people, people who had sat for portraits in my sketch book, most of them smiling faces, were looking at me, bragging to their neighbours about having their suspicions a long time ago. Like they knew all along.

You can imagine that since then, I've steered clear of a lot of white people. Rich or poor, it doesn't matter. Call me a racist, I don't care. I am too scared. I am too Black to be having that conversation around the water cooler about weaseling my way out of a speeding ticket by giving puppy eyes to a traffic officer. It doesn't work that way for me.

So that night, on Christmas Eve several months later when I saw the greasy-haired white guy at Mr Park's corner store near my town-house, I had that same feeling of dread. Palms. Ears. Chest. Back of my tongue. I kept my head down while I searched the shelves for popcorn. Mom wanted to watch some movies on TV for Christmas Eve.

Between two cylinders of Pringles potato chips on the shelf, I watched him stumble. He was wearing one of those black silk bomber jackets. You know, the ones from the nineties. Maybe he was a skinhead or something, back in the day.

He held hard onto the handles of the refrigerator section. He looked intensely at the contents. Gatorade. Cola. Butter. Then he slowly made his way to the cookie aisle. I could tell from the way he was looking at Mr Park behind the counter and at the packages of cookies, he was trying to assess which package he could stuff into his sleeve. I'm sure the guy would have been an expert at it had he been sober. But he wasn't. He looked at the package of Oreos. He looked at his sleeve. Then he saw a small bag of Hershey's Kisses and tried to slip it into his sleeve.

"Excuse me, sir?" Mr Park rolled his eyes. It was the worst shoplifting ever.

"What?"

"I can see you from here. Put that down and please leave."

"What? I can't look at things?"

"You weren't looking. You were stealing. Put it down. Get out."

"What?" The guy made this spitting noise, as if Mr Park was out of his mind imagining things. Dribble spurted from the side of his mouth. "I was looking for beer. I wasn't even looking for this. What are you talking about?"

I found Mom's popcorn but made sure not to make any noise with the box in my hand. I looked up at the round security mirror located above the refrigeration aisle to get a better view. Mr Park was shaking his head no, then his eyes met mine for a brief moment.

"The beer store is next door."

"Don't you speak English?"

"Beer store is next door."

"It's closed. You fucking chink." His voice broke. Like he was about to cry. "I was fucking there just yesterday ... I bought beer, but I didn't buy groceries ... Thought everything would've been open tonight. I don't even have the money to buy it all. That was my plan ... So stupid." He looked down at the bag of Hershey's Kisses in his hand and put it messily on the shelf beside loaves of bread. One loaf fell to the floor.

"Get out." Mr Park was trying to be both calm and firm.

The white guy swiped his arm across the shelf, making all the bread land on the floor.

"Leave now!"

He swiped his arm again, this time the chocolate bars in their boxes. He caught me looking at him.

"What are you looking at?"

I didn't answer. I quickly made my way to Mr Park. I placed four dollars on the counter, even though I knew the popcorn cost just over three dollars. I didn't want any trouble. I just wanted out of there. I headed to the door. The door's bell echoed behind me.

"Hey, buddy! You with the baggy jeans."

I wasn't wearing baggy jeans.

"What are you looking at?"

The white dude tapped me on the shoulder. I could smell the beer on his breath even though I was facing away from him.

"Hey! I'm talking to you!"

I pretended not to hear him. I began making my way home to the complex off Kingston Road.

"Hey, nigger! I'm talking to you!" he called out. As I crunched my way through snow and ice, out of the side of my eye I could see him lighting his cigarette clumsily, like an old lady trying to light birthday candles without her reading glasses on.

"Yeeow!" He'd singed the tips of his fingers and dropped his Bic lighter. He fumbled for it on the ground while still addressing me. "Wait!" He crouched down on his haunches. I don't know how he was able to do that with as much drink as he had in him.

I kept walking, looking back every now and then to be sure he wasn't following me.

LADY

Being a parent when your children are sleeping is both a blessing and a curse. A blessing because kissing your kids while they be dreaming is like ... I don't even know how to explain it. It's like your child is an old painting. One beautiful enough to hang on the wall. You just stare at it for as long as the clock will allow, watching their tummy rise and fall, rise and fall. My baby, I can see her pulling in her bottom lip, dreaming of suckling a mom who isn't even there.

A curse because ... well ... I receive texts from my mom to tell me Evan did this today, Yanna did that today. Maybe a picture if she figures out how to operate her phone camera in time. And here I am, stuck doing the Christmas Eve shift as a new nurse at Scarborough General's ER.

That night, I kissed my kids goodbye in time to leave for work. Yanna sleeps with her bum up to the ceiling. I gave it a pat and stroked her curly hair. I turned to Evan. He sleeps like a dead person. How he can share a room with a crying baby, I can never understand. I found him half off the bed. His pyjamas were twisted on his waist. I rolled him back into place and tucked his blanket into the side of the bed farthest from the wall in the hope that he wouldn't fall again. Tasha, my baby girl, lay perfectly still with her soother in her mouth. I carefully pried the soother out with my index finger and silently placed it beside the picture of their father. I pretend he is a good man, just not here. They believe me, just because of this picture.

My mom, who prefers the couch to my lumpy mattress, was still asleep. I could see the outline of her tired body, thanks to the glow of our mini-Christmas tree. I unplugged it just to be safe. My mother's ashy-looking foot and gnarly toenails stuck out of the blue felt blanket. As was my ritual, I touched her feet. A thank you.

I was running late. No time to deal with my hair, so I wrapped it tightly in my favourite peacock blue scarf. Without making a sound, I grabbed my keys, turned the deadbolt, and headed out. I could barely see straight, I was so damn tired after the kids opened all their presents and such. In another world, I would have slept this afternoon. But no such luck for a single mama.

I pressed the sticky down button for the elevator. The light behind the button never works, but this night was different. The round plastic knob glowed orange, like a warning. Something in my stomach told me to go back. I felt like I'd forgotten something. My phone? My keys? My ID card? It made no sense. But I went back to our apartment.

It was dark and quiet. I looked around. My mom's ashy foot. Kids sleeping quietly in the bedroom. Soother by the picture of my ex. What did I forget? I turned to the door and saw the wall.

The wall was glowing red. Like a burner on a stove. I smelled the smoke.

"Mom!"

"What is it, Lady?"

"Mom! Get the kids up. There's a fire!"

I remember the frenzy of grabbing the kids. They were like dead weights, they were so deeply asleep. Their heads bobbed from side to side.

"Lord!" my mom said while scrambling for her glasses and winter boots.

"Wake up! Wake uuup! Evan! Yanna! Wake up!"

My mom and I had to carry them. Mom, who has arthritis, took baby Tasha in her arms, wrapped in a blanket. Me, I carried Yanna like a monkey—facing me, her legs sleepily wrapped around my waist. Evan, I almost dragged him by his arms. I just couldn't carry both. Evan walked, one foot in front of the other, eyes half closed.

"Fire! FIRE! FIRE!" No one was listening. I could see smoke coming from next door, from underneath the space between carpet and doorframe. I could see it. I banged on the door. I tried the knob, and it burned my hand.

"OW!" I looked at the red welt on my hand. It smoked. No sound from inside the apartment.

"FIIIRE!" I banged on a couple of doors. When I think back, I wish I'd banged on a couple more. I think about that all the time. But what really got me was that there was no sound other than my voice. The cops tell me it's my imagination, but I know. I know I didn't hear anything. I know this. I'm not some fool who can hear my own voice but not the fire alarm. There was no fire alarm. It was just me, banging on doors.

"FIIIRE!"

Mom and I went to the nearest stairwell to head down to the ground floor. There were more and more tenants in their pyjamas. Joining us in the stairwell.

"FIIIRE!"

We began to bottleneck at the bottom.

"Everyone, just calm down!"

"Get out of our way!"

"Everyone out! Hurry!"

"Mommy, what's happening?!"

Outside, Christmas lights blinked on and off on the balconies while water was hosed onto the building. We all stood outside, our jaws dropped, watching the firemen douse the flames, most tenants in pyjamas that were flapping in the freezing wind, waiting for news.

IVANA

Our apartment complex would never be on a tourist pamphlet, that's for sure. Now, if you were to Google our address, you'd find us on the watch list for bed bugs in Toronto Community Housing. You'd also most likely find that famous photo of an old lady in curlers on her fifth floor balcony, dropping beer bottles on the heads of the cops for arresting her crack dealer. I never complain, though. It's so close to work.

Between happy endings at Oasis Spa, I can go out for a smoke at the back of the building and look up at my own balcony. See what's happening. If anyone is breaking in. It's better than an alarm system, not that I have anything to steal. I have to do so on the down-low, though. Not make a big deal of my suspicions, or even be seen much. I keep to myself, as a lot of my clients live in the same complex.

One snowy night, I noticed the girl. It was quiet. And there she was, looking out at the snow and at me. Reminded me of my days in Parkdale, near downtown. My mom and I lived in a huge house for little rent before the hipsters crowded everything out. There was even a fireplace and marble floors. It was big enough I could ride my tricycle in the foyer. Someone rich once lived there, for sure. I would ride my tricycle around on the marble floors of the kitchen and along the hardwood floors leading to my mom's room, where she would lie in bed for hours and ask me not to bother her. All I could see was a hand hanging limply outside the covers. The room had a huge bay window facing King Street. On days when my mom's depression hit,

I would spend hours watching the streetcar go back and forth. Back and forth. Sometimes the streetcar driver would ring his bell as he passed. It made me so happy.

I waved to the girl that night. It became a regular thing. I would try to find her every night when I was working and wave to her. Just like that streetcar driver. Maybe I was also making her happy.

On Christmas Eve, I had the night off. I went out to get more cigarettes at Tarek's convenience store. On my way back, I looked up the side of the building to see if the girl was there. Third floor. Window dark. No girl. I lit up to buy myself some time. I took a drag and let the smoke draw pictures around my face. No girl.

I finished my entire cigarette outside facing her balcony, in the freezing cold. I waited and waited. I'm not sure why I waited so long. I guess I knew she was in there. Just not at the window. I would have called her name if I knew it.

I only knew her name after she had died, and the news was all over the *Scarborough Mirror*. Laura Mitkowski.

BING

O Canada! Our home and native land! ...

The anthem played, as it always did, each and every single day. Standing before the perforated white square, we heard Celine Dion's voice, muffled and nasal through the circa 1980s PA system. All of us, our shoulders sagging and sad, let our ears ring with the familiar sound.

It was the first day back from Christmas holidays. If things were as usual, we would all be wearing our holiday presents. New jeans. New sweaters. New indoor shoes. New hairbands. Instead, we were wearing black ribbons pinned to our lapels. I fingered the sharp edge of my lapel pin with the skin of my thumb, positioning it so that it wouldn't pierce my chest by accident.

The microphone was adjusted on the PA system causing feedback.

"Good morning, Rouge Hill," said Mrs Rhodes, the coolie hat collector. I could tell by the way her voice was wavering, she was doing that white people thing when tragedy hits. She held the sorrow in her throat, hard and tight. "As many of you know, a sad event occurred during the holidays. Laura Mitkowski, who attended Mrs Landau's grade one class, is no longer with us." A long pause. A gulp. The microphone was adjusted again. "Her father, Cory Mitkowski, also perished." A pause. "Although many of us are sad that the fire that consumed their apartment took them from us, we are very happy that the other children at Rouge Hill who live in the same building survived and are here today attending class."

The microphone was adjusted yet again. A bit of a knock was heard on the apparatus. A couple more knocks.

"Thank you." It was a different voice now, from the background.

"*Boozhoo*," the voice continued, and it sounded like an old lady. A changing of the guard. We could hear Mrs Rhodes blow her nose. "My name is Elder Fay. *Boozhoo* means hello in my language, Ojibwa. I wanted to let you know I have come here to be your auntie today. All of you. Today I will be your moms, your aunties, and your grandmothers. I know a lot of us here are very sad about the news of Laura."

Sylvie stood beside me, her legs twisting, her shoulders convulsing in sobs.

"But we will meet today to talk things out, so that we can all know Laura is going to be okay."

A pipe ceremony was going to be held in the library. The hallways were foggy with the sweet smell of smudge. In the classrooms, in the locker rooms, in the staff room, winter sun painted the smoke into brush strokes. Our shuffling was solemn and quiet as we made our way to the library. Using their tissue-holding hands, the teachers with their red-eyed faces ushered us into concentric semicircles around Elder Fay. We sat obediently, criss-cross applesauce, on the faded carpet. Shoulders heavy. Faces wet. Even Aiden and Cole were crying, wiping away snot from their faces. Sylvie and I sat next to each other holding hands. Her hands were always sweaty.

Elder Fay sat quietly and patiently with a quilted blanket draped over her legs, her old eyes blinking away age and nearsightedness. Once everyone was seated, she began.

"Our friend Laura had seven years in this life. She got to see lots of things. And she got to meet a lot of you and make friends. She was a beautiful girl. But the Creator said it was time to go, and this can be very sad. It's okay to feel sad."

"Now, look what I have here." Elder Fay took out an eagle feather and put it down on a table next to the burning sage and all of her pipe implements. "I will put our friend the eagle feather here to watch over us and help us in our pipe ceremony." The non-Indigenous kids moved from side to side to watch. The Indigenous kids stared into the distance, something familiar. She began to put tobacco into the pipe. "I will smoke it for you. And my friend here," she indicated Levy, from grade six, sitting beside her, "he is going to help me light the pipe."

Levy had a brown square poker face and a closely shaven head, save for a braid running down the back of it. Although he was diminutive, he knew the protocol well. He took the matches from Elder Fay's table. Solemnly and with eyes at half mast, he expertly struck the red-tipped match against the side of the box and placed it over the pipe. Elder Fay drew in the fire, and it became smoke.

I imagined Laura in her apartment, the smoke filling the room. Trying to wake her father. In Cory's dreams, he was camping under the stars.

"While I am smoking, you can all help by thinking good thoughts about Laura, okay?"

I closed my eyes, doing as Elder Fay told me to, and thought good thoughts of Laura. I remembered her eating haw flakes with me and Sylvie. I remembered her dancing in her fairy costume. I remembered her at the snack table, eating Cheerios. I remembered her trying to teach me jump rope. I remembered Ms Hina and all of our parents lifting the parachute blanket up high to catch air so we could pretend it was a house or a spaceship. I remembered Laura touching the parachute fabric, laughing and running around me. I remembered her and her dad walking out of the school before the holidays, and her looking back at me and waving. I remembered her well.

That afternoon, when I came home from school, I snuck into Ma's dresser drawer to retrieve the Ziploc bag of Pa's foot tracings. I hid in my room and placed the paper foot outlines on the floor. Size 10, Florsheim shoes. His favourite. I placed my chubby, size-four feet over them, no socks. So much further to go.

DAILY REPORT

January 3, 2012

Facilitator: Hina Hassani

Location: Rouge Hill Public School

Attendance:

Parent/Guardian/ Caregiver	**Children** (one per line please)
Marie Beaudoin	Sylvie Beaudoin
	Johnny Beaudoin
Edna Espiritu	Bernard Espiritu
Helen McKay	Finnegan Everson
	Liam Williams
Fern Donahue	Paulo Sanchez
	Kyle Keegan
Natalia Angelo	Marca Angelo

Notes:

It was a very sad day here at the centre. I kept looking at the attendance sheet, wishing Cory was going to show up with Laura. I still can't believe they're both gone. Had a few tears during circle time, to be honest. All the kids and I were feeling it. I saw Laura every day here at the centre. So we were very close, although she rarely said a word. She just watched me make snacks every day. The funeral is scheduled for this Saturday, and

Laura's teacher, Mrs Landau, and I will be there for support. Since I have not used any of my sick days or mental-health days, I will do so next Monday. I will most definitely need it. I will fill out an official online request, as per protocol.

Weekly supplies requested:

2% milk	three bags, please
crackers	one box
cream cheese	one tub
apples	one bag

Jane Fulton <jfulton@ontarioreads.ca>
January 4, 2011
12:00 p.m. (4 hours ago)
To <hhassani@ontarioreads.ca>

Hi, Hina:
Thanks so much for letting us know the na-
ture of recent events. I saw the news and
couldn't believe it myself. I mentioned
this at your performance review, but perhaps it needs mentioning again: All daily reports need to focus on the details of
attendance, outreach actions on our behalf,
and activities done with the kids. I know
it is tempting to make the notes section
personal. If this seems like a challenge,
we can discuss over coffee sometime soon. My
door is always open. Just let me know when.
    As well, I want to caution you that com-
munity members are always in need, and it
can be hard to draw a line with them. Try
to keep personal lives out of the picture.
Remember, your focus is family literacy, not social work. I know there are grey
areas, and I appreciate the emotions that
you lovingly put into the centre. But if
we don't draw the line, our hearts can be
hurt a million times over, and we start to
do things such as booking off mental health
days. If you need some skill-building to
support you, we can chat anytime.
    I have received your request to take Mon-

day off, and I propose that we discuss some
strategies for you rather than you taking
time from the all-important work you do in
the community. I will be making my rounds
to visit the centres in the east district
regions, so I can drop by the centre this
Monday, perhaps around 11:00 a.m.
Take care!
Jane Fulton, MSW
Supervisor, Ontario Reads Program
Reading is a way for me to expand my mind,
open my eyes, and fill up my heart.
  —Oprah Winfrey

Me <hhassani@ontarioreads.ca>
January 4, 2011
2:00 p.m. (2 hours ago)
To Jane Fulton <jfulton@ontarioreads.ca>

Jane,
Thanks for your feedback.
   To be honest with you, I am appalled
by your email. One of the children in our
centres has died in a house fire. I think
there must be people in this community who
perhaps only brushed shoulders with the
Mitkowski family once or twice who are
shedding more tears than you.
   This is a tragic loss. And I am deeply saddened by it. I have a right to feel
those feelings and to take a mental health
day. And no, I will not discuss these

feelings with you over coffee during my
free time.

In future, I will reserve my notes for
logistical, statistical, cold-hearted information for your funding and development
officer, but today is a different day, and I
hope you understand.

Laura was not a news item to me, Jane.
She was a child. And we failed her. We all
failed her. And you are failing her again
by asking me to feel nothing.

Sincerely,
Hina Hassani, Facilitator
Ontario Reads Program, Rouge Hill Public
School

Ryan Hoffman <rhoffman@ontteachersuniondistrict10.ca>
January 6 2011 8:35 a.m. (2 hours ago)
To <hhassani@ontarioreads.ca>

Hina Hassani,
Thank you for your call to our union and
for your email message. I apologize for not
getting back to you yesterday, as my family and I had just returned from our trip to
New Orleans.

As your union representative, I have reviewed the series of messages between you
and your supervisor, Jane Fulton, and there
is definitely cause for concern. We do have
a pretty strong case re: Islamaphobic com-

ments about your hijab and re: breaking
contract rules by expecting you to do outreach beyond your work week and not granting you a mental health day following the
death of one of the centre's children.

Can you give me a shout at the office? I
have a district union meeting at 3 p.m.,
but it should be done in an hour. We can
talk in detail and perhaps set up a meeting with your management to talk about re-
course.

In the meantime, please draft me a basic
timeline of your interactions with Ms. Fulton. I would like further details about her
criticism of your attendance at the child's
funeral. Please know that attending the funeral of one of your students is *not*, by any
means, crossing a line. In fact, I am certain
that management did not follow protocol re: trauma to its staff, which would
include a student death.

Anyway, please give me a call this after-
noon, and we can chat more.
Ryan Hoffman, District 10 Representative
United Teacher's Union of Ontario

PART 3

SPRING

The sound of ice cracking and rivers flowing. The Rouge conservation area is alive again. Three fawns travel like secrets through the forest at sunset.

At the corner of Markham Road and Lawrence Avenue
Elders are finally able to brave the slightly warmer weather to show-case their wares. Expansive hooked rugs with images of lions on them. Bed sheets dedicated to the memory of Bob Marley. Who buys them? No one knows.

On Starspray Boulevard
Ravinder Kaur happily puts a sold sticker on a sale sign. Another house sold to another brown family in an otherwise white neighbour-hood.

Evalyn Chau <echau@ontarioreads.ca>
February 12 2011 9:40am (4 hours ago)
To <hhassani@ontarioreads.ca>

Hello, Hina:

My name is Evalyn Chau, and I am the successor to Mrs Jane Fulton, your former supervisor. I want to extend a warm greeting to you as I enter my new position. I am aware of the unfortunate circumstances in which Mrs Fulton was dismissed and the details re: the disagreement between you. I want to express my heartfelt sadness that such discrimination would take place. I also want to get to know you and to ensure that we start our relationship as supervisor-facilitator off on the right foot!

I have read in great detail the numerous letters sent to the union in response to the situation with Mrs Fulton. As you may know, community members living in the Kingston/Galloway area who you have served at the centre this school year wrote letters in support of your character and your positive effect on their lives. I was moved to tears.

I have seen numerous signed petitions in support of a change in policy. But the fully written letters in support of your case against Mrs Fulton are noteworthy.

One letter in particular had my attention with every word.

To Whom It May Concern:
My name is Marie Beaudoin and I, along
with my children Sylvie and Johnny,
attend the literacy centre regularly.
This centre is located within the Rouge
Hill Public School.

I could tell you that we attend the
centre because I need a place for my
youngest, Johnny, to play, especially
since he has developmental issues.

But truthfully, we use it as a place
to be normal and to have something
to eat, mainly breakfast, so that my
Sylvie can attend class with a full
stomach.

When I met Ms Hina the first time, I
was scared she may judge me for having
these two hungry kids. But she never
has.

Sylvie's favourite breakfast is
Crispix cereal, and Ms Hina always
ensures she's stocked up for us.

Being First Nations, we have enjoyed
that there are at least three books
in Ojibwa on the shelf. This is not
our language, as I am Mi'kmaq, but it
really matters to me that there are
some books my kids can relate to.

We live in a shelter. This means it
never feels right to put anything any-
where, because it's not home yet.

But at the centre, Ms Hina always makes sure Sylvie can put her paintings up, and she's welcome to the toys like they're hers.

I know the disagreement between Ms Hina and her manager was because she felt Ms Hina was getting too personal with the folks here.

The truth is you can't NOT get too personal with us. And let me tell you, there is DRAMA! Can't help it. It's Scarborough (lol).

Ms Hina is a very kind person who loves her job. Most importantly, she is honoured to do her job. Heck, I'm not honoured to be a parent sometimes. But Ms Hina is honoured to know us. Hardly anyone out here is honoured to know us folks. Most of us are dirt poor, and our parents are embarrassed by us. But Ms Hina is different.

I want to tell you to call me if you have any questions, but I don't have a phone (lol). I guess you can see me at the centre if you want to discuss this letter with me.

Sincerely,
Marie Beaudoin

Hina, I applaud you for earning such a

letter and for cultivating such meaningful
relationships. You're doing exactly what
you're supposed to be doing.

I see that you are attending the workshop re: introverted and extroverted children at the Professional Development Day
next Friday. Can I treat you to lunch that
day?

Great job, and bye for now.

Sincerely,
Evalyn

BING

School was closed for the day, which meant I got to spend my time with Ma at the nail salon. Usually this excites me because it means I'm in charge of disinfecting all the implements. All the estheticians hand me their dishes filled with nail clippers and files. I wash them, imagining I'm a surgeon rescuing a man with a bullet wound to the chest.

"Forceps!" I say to myself and pass the cuticle cutter from latex-gloved hand to latex-gloved hand.

This day, however, was different. I put the tools into the mildew-stained tool oven to kill off the germs and waited for the timer to go off, my head heavy on my palm. I didn't even want to go out back to say hello to Ivana.

"*Anak!*" Ma called from the salon. I came out obediently to find Miss Peaches. "Look who's here! Say hello."

Miss Peaches is a buxom, voluptuous Trini woman whose hair looks different each time she visits us to get her acrylics filled. She is one of Ma's regulars. Her usual monologues about the pressure for her to get married and have a baby are silenced under Ma's foot massages. Miss Peaches is the only client Ma doesn't rush. No bad energy, Ma explained to me one day.

Miss Peaches beckoned me to her, as she often does. I took off my *tsinelas* and stepped up on the tiled platform to meet her, eye to eye, as she sat in the pedicure chair, its back massager whirring.

"Hello, my little man." She took both my hands in hers, rubbing the tops of them with bejewelled thumbnails. Tender, loving. "How you be?"

"Monday is his test for the gifted program. The teacher knows how smart he is." Ma ran her fingers through my hair, brushing my overgrown tresses to the side. She then put on her latex gloves and got to work on Miss Peaches' feet.

"Of course you are. You are so smart."

I wilted and looked at the tiles. I didn't feel like smiling.

"Hey. Look at me." Miss Peaches took her index nail and tilted my head up to peer into my eyes. Behind all the adornment, I knew she was magic. "You are a special boy. You see how hard your mommy is working?"

Ma peered up for a second behind her mask. Her eyes met mine for a moment, then she looked down to continue her work, exfoliating and filing.

"You have to work very hard so that your mommy doesn't have to work that hard anymore. You will show them how smart you are. You just be you. When you show everyone how special you are, your life will change. For you. For your mommy. Always take care of your mommy."

Ma looked up at me, her eyes moist above her mask. "Bing took care of me already." I knew what she was saying. She remembered that day we left Daddy, and it was me who held her hand when we left Moss Park.

As soon as the doors of Pearson Memorial Junior Public School swung open, I knew I was in one fancy establishment. The hallways were empty, meaning everyone was in class, unlike at Rouge Hill, where the lineup to the principal's office was long and adversarial.

"You need to drop off your child at 8:45 a.m.," the Rouge Hill secretary would say while scribbling on yellow late slips and handing them to tired working parents. They would rub their tired eyes with stained hands and say nothing.

At Pearson Memorial Junior Public School, Ms Hina's hand was a familiar sensation walking through these foreign corridors. In one classroom a girl projected a presentation on a screen from an iPad. A flock of animated seagulls flew across the screen to show the words "The End," in handwritten font. As the girl bowed deeply to her class's applause, her eyes met mine as we passed by.

From another classroom, children repeated phrases in singsong French. The kindergarten class had the most expensive rain boots lined up outside, and paper bumblebees on the wall above marked the name of each owner. Inside the classroom, the kids worked on a giant mural, and their teacher happily took pictures of them.

"Ms Hina?" I looked up at her slender figure walking beside me.

"Yes, Bing."

"If I do good today, do I get to come here?" I was hopeful and felt ashamed for being so. Ms Hina stopped in her tracks and knelt down to meet my eye.

"Hey, how you do here can't be bad. They're doing something called assessing. It means they are just trying to figure out what kind of school will be best for you. Some kids have special needs.

And I think you have a special need, meaning you need more challenging schooling to make it fun. Does that make sense?"

My face was hot. I knew my brown cheeks had turned pink.

"So just answer the questions the best you can. Okay?" I could tell she was nervous too. As much as everyone was telling me about this assessment, I know they knew it meant something better for me. Because no matter how much people called it a special need, it happened to be one that was celebrated.

"Hello, Bernard," said Mrs Rhodes. She stood up from a long table. A white man in a suit sat opposite her and did not rise. "This is Mr Palmer. He will be here to help me today."

Mr Palmer smiled faintly, flipped the paper on his clipboard.

"Do you know why you're here?" said Mrs Rhodes in a way that I knew she was about to answer her own question. "Mrs Hina and Mrs Finnegan both feel that you may be eligible for the gifted program. So today we are going to do some tests, to see if you think in a way that may mean you need another program to help you feel more challenged and excited about school."

I remember images in a flipbook with thick black wire binding. I remember blocks put before me, which I had to rearrange to match a photo. I remember being asked questions about my perception of the placement of things. Of right and wrong. I remember thinking of my mother's hand in mine during that drive to Scarborough so long ago.

That night, after my test, my mom held me so hard, kissing my hair with pressed lips. Her Filipino kisses. Ninety-ninth percentile. If I was in a room with ninety-nine other children the same age as me, they would consider me smarter than ninety-nine of them. I was going to the gifted program.

SYLVIE

My daddy told me about when his dog died. On the New Brunswick Atlantic shore, near my grandpa's trailer. He was walking Hot Dog. It was one of those nasty winters, one that keeps folks wearing their fleeces and longjohns well into the summer, just in case. It was full of blackouts and floods, ice storms and frost quakes. My daddy lost his grip on his troubled beagle in the midst of a snowstorm. Not much visibility past your toes. When recalling the story, Daddy waves his arms to and fro, eyes still squinting at the memory.

You see, Hot Dog was a puppy mill survivor. Probably had six litters before she was rescued. Had teats down to her ankles. Would never leave a crying baby. Would cry at the sight of people sun tanning, thinking they were dead. Was scared of life and of being left behind. Her wailing was horrible. Her leash discipline was even worse.

She came undone that winter night and ran. She loved running after years of being pent up in a kennel, forced to make babies. That night, she was free. That is, until she met the headlights of an oncoming southbound VIA Rail train.

My daddy didn't know that, though. For a whole week he went to the ocean shores, calling her name. One dusk, at the water's edge, he saw a deer. A buck, and his antlers were majestic. Magic. He made eye contact with my father, a silent message that would visit my father's dreams well into adulthood. He knew then, somehow, his dog was never coming back.

Daddy remembers the track worker who retrieved Hot Dog's remains from the site where her body was thrown. The worker reassured him—a helpless, sobbing child—that death had been quick.

On that Saturday when Bing led me away from the playground and our sunbathing moms to his secret place in Port Union Commons, I knew he was going to leave me. "Here." Bing held out his hand. I took it. Like my daddy's buck, he made eye contact with me and made a silent message between our palms. A realization. He led me through a graffiti-filled tunnel to the rocks and lake.

A white pagoda stood at the edge, waves crashing into the shore. Change. Inside the pagoda, a fresh patch of concrete and four orange barriers kept people from the wet surface. "Someone dug a hole here last summer, so they're repairing it," Bing told me. Bing crossed the orange barrier and took me with him. He gingerly touched the wet concrete.

"If we write our names, people hundreds of years from now will know we were here." You know someone is leaving when they start taking pictures with their minds of everything around them. And so we placed our hands in the wet concrete and wrote "Sylvie + Bing BFFs" in cursive as graceful as the concrete goop would allow.

We returned to the playground and pressed the button to turn on the sprinkler.

"You guys have fun by the lake?" my mama asked.

We laughed and screamed at the sensation of frigid water hitting our skin. We ran about, our baby fat jiggling under the hiss and spray. We watched in wonder as rainbows came and went, as clouds made hippo shapes on the concrete. We sat on the sprinkler with our bums and giggled at the sound. We laughed and laughed.

Christy was leaving, too.

"Good riddance," Mama said to me while sorting laundry. "That girl is on an express train to trouble."

Christy stood in the common area surrounded by a mish-mash of broken suitcases and liquor boxes full of her meagre belongings. One of them was marked "Sylvie."

"Hey, treasure hunter. You want any of these? Anything you don't want, you can just toss."

I looked inside. A sand dollar. I put it to my ear. "That isn't a shell you can hear the ocean with," laughed Christy, before her smoker's cough interrupted her.

A whistle. A measuring tape. A make-your-own-kite kit. I could tell these were new things she bought from the dollar store or something. My heart swelled and fell. Christy would be back at the shelter one day. Even at my young age, I have seen it so many times. Dads who lose their kids and then find Jesus. Single mamas with dozens of kids who think they have a room at their sister's house, but then plans change. And now Christy, skinny, slutty Christy, in love and moving in with Roy, pusher of weed and women, lover of drama and tattoos.

"Don't you want to hear the rest of the story?"

"Okay, Sylvie. But Roy will be here any minute. We're having a barbecue tonight in his—I mean our—apartment."

"Where were we?" I reached to pick my nose, as I usually did when I was thinking hard. Christy hooked her finger against mine to discourage it. She hated when I picked my nose.

"All the other animals began dropping objects into the orangutan compound."

In the window just behind Christy, I could see Roy reversing his beat-up Grand Caravan, ready for the move.

I began the story as fast as I could.

"Everyone knows that New Year's Eve is the biggest night at the zoo. All the kids and their parents go there for a fake countdown to midnight, when it's really just eight at night."

Christy was suddenly distracted by the sight of Roy. Her eyes danced.

I raised my voice so she could hear me. "So Clementine, along with her siblings, took the zookeepers' clipboards and tied them together with necklaces that the White Handed Gibbons snatched off of visitors. And they used a jacket and a mop handle for their sail."

Roy entered the shelter scrolling through text messages with one hand and side hugging Christy with the other. He was a scrawny red-headed man. Nothing like how I imagined him. His denim shirt was unbuttoned low enough to show his pepperoni-like nipples. Christy cradled into the bony edges of him.

I continued as Christy and Roy began to load the van, my voice as loud as possible.

"When the zookeepers and the visitors were counting down to midnight, the orangutans pushed their raft across the pool to the other side. Everyone gave them high-fives through their cages.

Some jumped up and down. Some splashed in their aquariums. But the Painted Box Turtles simply waved goodbye."

"Is that so?" Christy said, tossing a pair of broken heels into the garbage. "And where did they go? After leaving the zoo?"

"They went to Rouge Hill Campground."

"The one right over here? Near the bridge to Pickering?"

"Exactly," I said, glad to have her attention for one last moment. "They're there even now, sharing a two-bedroom trailer. They never made it to the rainforest, but they have lots of trees to climb. And since Scarborough is a sunrise place, they wake up every morning, enjoy tea, and watch the sky turn red."

Roy gave Christy a nod, then headed outside. He started the engine of the Grand Caravan and it roared Christy into attention.

"I've got to go, kiddo."

I held my box of treasures tightly. "Bye, Christy." My voice wavered.

Christy took one last look at me. She fingered the make-your-own-kite kit.

"You ever fly a kite before?" I shook my head. I have broken so many, but I didn't want her to know that. I have the worst luck with them. They always get caught in trees.

"The secret is to let the string go into the wind. You gotta feel with your hands when the moment is right, and let go."

Christy tousled my hair, believing she would never see me again.

"See you later, alligator." Then she left.

DAILY REPORT

April 23, 2012

Facilitator: Hina Hassani

Location: Rouge Hill Public School

Attendance:

Parent/Guardian/Caregiver	Children (one per line please)
Marie Beaudoin	Sylvie Beaudoin
	Johnny Beaudoin
Edna Espiritu	Bernard Espiritu
Helen McKay	Finnegan Everson
	Liam Williams
Fern Donahue	Paulo Sanchez
	Kyle Keegan
Natalia Angelo	Marca Angelo
Pamela Roy	Evan Roy
	Yanna Roy
	Tasha Roy

Notes:

Today was a lovely day. We were able to open the exterior door to the courtyard to let the air in and the kids out. I set up the water table outside so that the kids could splash about. Some of the caregivers even stripped them down to diapers, to avoid wet clothes. It was so funny.

Thank you, Evalyn, for sending me the news about the amalgamation of the literacy centres with the Provincial Play Centres. This isn't the first time I have been part of a program that comes and goes, but it doesn't make it any less of a heartbreak. Governments enter and exit, but we frontline workers are the ones who get lost in the shuffle. Actually, that's not true. It's our communities we work so hard for that get lost in the shuffle. I'm so glad you will be staying on to coordinate the programs, as I have had such a positive experience under your stewardship.

Anyway ... I want to express my interest in staying in this community if our program gets restructured. I understand there may be some shuffling between us at Rouge Hill Public School and those at East Side Early Play down the road. I don't want to see all the bridge-building I've done go to waste. Every day, I am inspired by these people's resiliency. Every day, I am honoured to know them all.

EDNA

I have long days.

The day started with a ten o'clock appointment with the cop. He always comes in on his days off. The first time I saw him was in uniform, about a year ago, when there was a shoplifter at Tarek's convenience store next door. I saw him through the window while I was sweeping toenails off the tiles, and he nodded his head at me. All the ladies at the rub and tug, Ivana and them, manage to stay out of his way each time he strolls along our strip mall. I think they have an understanding. I'm pretty sure he's a customer, and he enters their premises from the back.

"Good morning, Officer Tyndall," I said when he came in today, out of uniform. He nodded. He enjoys seeing me feel afraid of him. I had decided a long time ago to never really look him in the eye. Instead, my eyes were on the footbaths I was filling with bleach and warm water to start the day.

"You ready for me?" His face winced at the smell of bleach. This made me happy. He had scheduled a waxing appointment. This was different from his usual manicure, when, as I do with any client, I unbutton his shirt cuff to reveal his entire forearm. With my right hand, I pump lotion onto my fingers. Inevitably, the pump is only half full of dollar store-grade lotion. Inevitably, the lotion splatters across my thighs. Inevitably, Officer Tyndall says, "Ooooh, is this getting personal, Edna?" I do not respond. I begin massaging the sinew along his forearms, toward the bend of his elbows, and keep my eyes down to avoid seeing the creases of his lips upturned. Smirking at me. My thumbs make their way to his palms, making circles along his life-line. His smirk grows bigger. "If you can do this with my hands ... who knows what you can do elsewhere," he says. I do not respond. I never respond. And still, he always says it.

Today, he had asked for a back wax and headed to the facial rooms. I closed the door behind me. "My girlfriend likes me smooth all over, you know?" He started to remove his striped golf shirt, re-vealing a turtleneck of hair from the bottoms of his earlobes to above the crack of his bum. I shuddered.

I had not even finished rolling out the paper on the surface of the waxing bed, and he had flopped his body facedown, like a child waiting for his bedtime story and for me to tuck him in. I snapped my latex gloves into place. I checked the consistency of the wax by dipping a tongue depressor in and out of the pot. Like caramel. Hot caramel. I shook baby powder across his torso to make it look like Christmas. Then I began to apply the hot wax along the direction of hair growth. He moaned since I refused to cool the liquid down one bit. If he were a different client, I would have blown on the wax be-fore applying it. But I was enjoying his pain too much. Once he was covered from nape to crack, I began my torture. I chose the largest patches of linen strips I could find to begin the pulling process. From the small of his back I pressed the linen into the wax and pulled the hair from the root, like an ugly carpet in an ugly house that I wanted to demolish.

"Aaaaah! Ooooh!" He began screaming with every pull. And with every pull I thought of the times his knees made their way between my legs under the manicure table. "AAAAAH! YOWCH!" I thought of the times he leaned into me, to smell my ear. "SHIT! GOD, THAT HURTS!" I thought of all the times he handed me my one dollar tip and winked at me. "JESUS! PLEASE! IT HURTS! STOP!" I did not. I did not stop until he was as hairless as a newborn mouse. I turned him over and did it all over again on his chest. I noticed his eyes tearing up.

In the most singsong, docile voice, I said, "Oh, Officer Tyndall, are you crying?"

He buried his face into his elbow. "No."

Eleven o'clock was Mrs Zoe. She is one of my favourites. Just like all days, she came in with new hair. I told her I loved it. She thanked me. She sat down and placed her cellphone on the table in front of her while I filled her acrylics. Her look is the stiletto pointed, Thursday nail manicure, which means detailing on the ring finger. Today she chose fake crystals, with a chocolate base on her other digits. She does not know my name but knows I will be paired with her when she comes in. She likes my attention to detail. As per usual, we sat in complete silence while she scrolled through her Facebook page, and I lovingly placed crystals on her Thursday finger. I love the quiet, and she does, too. The other girls had clients who were filling the air with conversation. But Mrs Zoe, even as I massaged the black skin on the back of her hands, closed her eyes, enjoying the silence.

Two o'clock. An older lady with glasses and a fancy bag hanging from her arm came in, wanting a pedicure. "I don't want a varnish today. I want someone who is good at massage." I asked her if she at least wanted a topcoat, to make her toenails shiny. "No, really, I just want the nails cleaned and trimmed. The focus should be the massage."

After completing her pedicure, I dried her feet with my towel and positioned her soles facing me. Once I started the massage, the old lady began moaning in delight. She moaned and moaned like this was the first time she had ever been touched. Like she was seeing God. I looked up at her and saw that her glasses were askew. The touch was so pleasurable for her, and everyone in the spa could hear; I was surprised she didn't begin undressing.

"I will see you next week," said the old lady while fanning herself. She gave me a sly wink. I gulped.

By five o'clock, the girls and I had done about four pedicures each. The floor was littered and crunchy with nails and skin. Mae knew I wanted to finish work early, but I wasn't able to shake my last client, Mrs Fitz, who insisted I do her feet. I hated her and used our sessions to meditate on what I had done in my life to deserve such torture.

Mrs Fitz was buffed and painted, fast and furious. This did not stop her from going on about her mother-in-law during March break. She gesticulated here and there with her newly painted hands. Finally, she ended her lengthy story with a downward inflection and placed a cold toonie in my hands. She held them for a moment. Privileged, upper-class pampered paws enveloped my raw-skinned hands. *This is for you, and for your poor little family,* said the gesture. A longing look into my eyes, waiting for a thank you.

"Thank you, miss."

I hung up my apron, still littered with foot leather. From the corner near the sanitizer, I grabbed my newly purchased karaoke machine and tipped it on its side to allow the wheels to carry its weight. I tucked the mic with its extra-long cord wrapped in a haphazard bunch under my arm.

Mae and the other estheticians hadn't even turned on the "closed" sign at the nail salon, and I was speed walking south down Poplar Road as fast as my flip-flops would allow, face hot, the skin between my big and second toe tender from my sandals.

"Wait! Wait!" Mae called out. The estheticians marched down the street in a caravan of clip-clopping soles and giggles. Tonight was the night.

Ms Hina met me and the girls at the doors of the school. She directed Mae and the girls to the ticket desk before shuffling me and my karaoke machine with its cassette tape deck to the back of the school gym. Past blue eye shadow and tulle skirts. Past polyester suits and frilly cummerbunds. Past matching jumpsuits and high top sneakers. Past crying kids suffering from stage fright. Past parents double-fisted with ice cream cones, hoping their kids would perform "Pearly Shells" on demand. Past the faded mustard yellow heavy velvet curtain. To my handsome Bing, dressed in a black and white tuxedo, his hair expertly combed to the side.

Ms Hina gave us both a hug before she rushed off to attend to a vomiting child.

"Ready *ka na, anak*?" I bent over slightly to meet the eyes of my son. I realized I didn't need to bend over much. He was getting taller. Bing nodded silently.

I took both his earlobes between my thumbs and forefingers.

Like I've always done when he gets nervous. Bing noticed my ivory bracelets were missing. He circled my wrists with his fingers, like placeholders. He looked at the new karaoke machine and realized the truth.

I changed the subject quickly. "Listen, ha? You need to relax. Tita Mae is out there. The whole gang is out there. Just have fun. We will be cheering for you."

I held my son and kissed his gel-stiff hair. Then I turned to the karaoke machine and put the volume up to maximum. I turned the vocal track dial down all the way to one, then plugged the machine into a dusty outlet behind the curtain.

The gym doors were open to cool the humid room. The multi-coloured sports pennants on the wall drooped like felt pizzas in the heat. Parents were fanning themselves to no avail. They moving squeakily from one bum cheek to another, partly to keep themselves awake, partly to drown out the sound of the tone-deaf band. Nothing could help these kids: not the flailing arms of their teacher, not the encouraging smiles of parents behind cameras. When the screeching was over, there was uproarious applause, for the mediocrity was finally done. The curtain closed just shy of a music stand that a disembodied arm retrieved. Shuffles. Whispers. Stampede of adolescent feet to the wings.

The curtain opened with heavy increments of swish and slide, thanks to the scrawny arms of a small boy in Coke-bottle glasses. He gestured for Bing to go to centre stage. Bing obliged with karaoke machine in tow. Once he hit his mark, the squeaking of the machine's wheels was replaced by the familiar hiss of a tape deck and the click of a microphone switch. Bing turned his tuxedo tails to the audience. I held my breath. For once the gym was silent.

The music began. Whitney Houston. Eighties synth. Drum kit. From the echo-filled mic, Bing began to sing. He whipped his body around to the audience, and I was stunned to realize the falsetto voice was coming from my boy. I looked around the gym. Faces were curious, putting two and two together.

Like a war cry, Bing sang a high lick while simultaneously ripping off his tuxedo jacket.

"*Naaaks namaaan!*" I screamed from the audience. Mae and all the gals from the nail salon stood up and cheered.

"Go, Bing!"

Parents found themselves applauding. Bing motioned for the audience to clap along. His shoulders pumped up and down to the downbeat. His hips swayed expertly from side to side. His beautiful voice echoed off the walls. Bounced off washroom stalls. Off glass cases and the trophies inside.

Just like we rehearsed, Bing began to undo his bowtie while gyrating his hips.

"Is this too much, Ma?" he asked me when we rehearsed. "I think people will make fun of me."

"You will never be too much. You will never be too little, Bernard. You be you."

The crowd was in hysterics. They sang along, a song they knew so well sung by a boy they had not understood. He tore off his button-up shirt and threw it to the floor. I caught myself doing the gestures I had helped choreograph. Just at the climax, he revealed his bedazzled pink halter top. Triumph.

I could not swallow my tears any longer. The warm salty water streamed down my face into the folds of my neck. It felt so good to see him display for all to see the magic I saw every day. This was my son. Beyond sainthood. Beyond Jesus. Beyond survival. Beyond lipstick. Beyond singing in the mirror. This was my son. My beautiful child.

The crowd rose to their feet, clapping and screaming.

Bing's face was covered with sweat as he raised his arm in the air, striking his final pose. Standing ovation, prolonged applause.

I could see everyone clapping but could not hear it past my sobs. This is joy. All those hours working. Pulling hair. Shirking sexual advances. Feigning gratitude for one-dollar tips. How lucky am I to do so, to ensure the security of this child? How lucky am I to do this, in the name of mothering this magical person? How lucky am I to have been chosen by God to be this boy's mother?

BING

"Is this too much, Ma?" I asked, holding up the Whitney Houston cassette tape. "I think people will make fun of me."

"You will never be too much. You will never be too little, Bernard. You be you." My heart fluttered hearing her say that.

"Really?" I sat cross-legged amongst the other cassette tapes, all possible song choices for the school talent show. None of the songs were newer than 1995. They were all Mom's tapes, from her days growing up in Cavite, back in the Philippines. "What about Michael Jackson?"

"Everyone does Michael Jackson." Ma continued sewing pink sequins on my halter top. She repositioned her ivory bracelets higher on her forearm so they wouldn't clink.

"Frank Sinatra?"

"You are performing for children. Not the old folks' home." We giggled. "*Anak*, why not Whitney Houston? Why are you doubting yourself?"

"Because Whitney is a girl."

"So?"

"People will say I shouldn't sing it because I'm a boy."

Ma held my face. "You're so much more than a boy, Bing." My eyes welled up. I thought for a second I would tell her about the kiss Hakim and I shared, but I didn't want to ruin the moment. "Tell me. What, in your own words, is this song about?"

"She really wants to dance. And she hopes the person she likes will dance with her."

"Have you ever wanted to dance with somebody?" My face grew hot. She poked my soft tummy. "Ha? Have you?" I smiled shyly and folded my hand over her fingers. It tickled.

"Yes, Ma."

"Okay. See? Then does it matter if you're a boy or girl?"

"No, Ma." I held up the cassette tape. "But how will we play this? Our tape deck isn't loud enough." I pointed to our outdated boom box with intermittently dysfunctional speakers.

"Just relax, ha? I will figure things out."

She used her teeth to cut the fuchsia thread and held the halter top against my torso. "Looking good. Okay, try it on, and we can test the tuxedo."

I did as I was told. First, the halter top. She helped me slip the sleeves of my white shirt on from behind, then the tuxedo jacket. I felt like one of those bullfighters in Spain that I saw in a documentary once. It was like a ritual, putting on all the special gear while the family looks on, watching and crying. That was my mom, getting all teary eyed dressing me up. Her little fighter.

"You know, you remind me of your Tito Ferdie. He was brave, like you. I knew he was different when we played together." I thought about Tito Ferdie lying in his casket while we prayed his soul away. "He even had a boyfriend, you know? Or girlfriend. I don't know what you would call him. At the funeral, he stood to the side and cried. He cried and cried and cried. We all pretended he wasn't there." She looped the bowtie around my neck and began tying it into a perfect bow. "I wish I was brave like you and had said hello to him. To show him I could see him. To show him I cared."

She wiped her tears away, then repositioned me in front of our hallway closet mirror. We both looked at my reflection, satisfied. Ma nodded her head, her bottom lip pursed and proud.

"Wow, *naman*. Okay. Are you ready?" I nodded yes. I grabbed the lapels of my tuxedo jacket and pulled. The Velcro she sewed into the back seams busted loose perfectly. I tossed it to the side.

"Now the shirt, Bing." I tore open the Velcro releases along the button front with ease. We high-fived each other.

I appreciated her embellishments to my costume. You always need a little help from Velcro. It's not like in the movies, when people rip their clothes off easily. I knew this, because my daddy once ripped my shirt and he almost choked me, trying. It was around that time he started chipping away at our apartment wall. "There's someone talking in there," he told us, inspecting each piece of drywall for a clue.

The day he ripped my shirt, he had asked me to remove a spike from the back of his neck. "It's there. It's there. Just look. Use your eyes, Bing." I looked. I did as he asked me. I touched his bare neck. I saw nothing.

"You have it, too! We all have it. Just take mine out, and I'll take out yours."

I cried, quietly. He flipped me around violently to look at the back of my neck. He tried to rip the back of my T-shirt off, searching for a spike that wasn't there. This tightened the collar around my neck, and I choked.

"Daddy! Daddy! No!" I managed to cough out.

He dropped me to the ground. Both of us were out of breath. His hand went to the back of his neck again, confused. He went into the washroom and did not leave until Ma came home hours later.

"So, what do you think?" Ma looked at my reflection and shifted the halter top.

"Thank you, Ma." I gave her a kiss. She looked at me like she could see the memory in my eyes and embraced me hard, the cool of her ivory bracelets on my cheeks.

The night of the performance, Ma massaged my earlobes like she always did when I was nervous. But something was different.

"Where are your bracelets?"

"What bracelets?"

I looked at the new karaoke machine at her feet. I looked at her empty wrists.

"Where did this come from?"

"Listen, ha? You need to relax. Tita Mae is out there. The whole gang is out there. Just have fun. We will be cheering for you."

Between knowing my mother sold her bracelets for me and the possibility I'd be beaten up for being a girl, I worried I'd made a mistake. Maybe Ma could still trade out the Whitney Houston cassette for the Frank Sinatra one. Maybe I could improvise my choreography. Maybe the audience would sing along loudly enough they wouldn't notice that I didn't know the lyrics.

But then the curtains slid open. I could feel the heat of the lights on my scalp. I switched the microphone on. Showtime. The music started. With my back still to the audience, I did chest isolations to the beat of the syncopated rhythm. It was like my ribs broke through something. Something like a wall. Something like the crash of waves.

My right hip joined in the isolations, up and down with the sound of the synth. And just as I began singing into the microphone, I expanded my chest—flat enough that you could place a coffee cup on it, Ma instructed—and pivoted around to face the audience.

There was no turning back now. Sweat dribbled down the end of my nose. I could hear from the speakers the sound of my feminine voice. My truth.

I could see confusion. The audience was wondering if I was lip syncing or singing. But my fancy trills confirmed everything. This was all me.

"*Naaaks namaaan!*" I heard Ma scream from the audience. I remembered the last time she screamed. "Liiiisssen, *anak*. We have to leave here. It's no longer safe."

I pumped my shoulders left and right. I pointed at stunned audience members. Ma had instructed me to walk along the lip of the stage with my hand extended to give high-fives to my adoring fans. But there were none. Just bewildered school band members. My voice cracked slightly at the thought of possible failure.

"Go to your room!" I remembered Daddy yelling at me after he had placed his hand in the hot frying pan on purpose. He held his blistering skin, screaming, "You ugly little boy. GO! Get out!"

Then the familiar chorus started. I gestured for everyone to clap along. They did. In waves, the adults got up from their seats and clapped too.

I grabbed the lapels on my tuxedo jacket, held my breath, and tugged hard. I threw it into the audience at Hakim who twirled it like a prize he'd just won. Everyone was standing and clapping to the beat.

It was time to take things down a notch with the bridge. I dropped to both knees, singing into the microphone as I wanted to sing into Hakim's ear. I sang of searching for a dance partner. Somebody to hold me. Somebody who loves me. The audience leaned in, wondering what was to happen next.

I remembered the trip to the zoo. "Open up your lunches. This beached whale needs to be fed." Aiden taunting me, as I cowered on the floor of the bus, helpless and crying.

Just as the chorus began again, I jumped to my feet, ripped off my button-up shirt and revealed my pink-sequined halter top. Everyone cheered. Under the auditorium lights, I felt the sweat on my bare arms both cooling and accumulating. Riding the wave of a sustained note, I felt my insides shine like a light beaming from my throat and through every finger. Truth. Truth. It felt like confetti. It felt like running. It felt like screaming. Me. Truth. Truth.

I ended with my fist in the air, my eyes closed. I could hear everyone on their feet, cheering for me. I could also hear my own breathing. Deep, like I was touching something way up high. The lights shone on my face. It felt so good to be me.

MARIE

Let me tell you something: Changing the dirty diaper of a three-year-old is no picnic in the park. It's more like a trip to Shitville, population: me. I remember those days when Johnny just lay there, when he was a newborn. I changed his tiny bum, with his tiny poop, and Sylvie helped her mama by handing me wipes. Johnny remained so perfectly helpless and still. He smelled so good in his onesie. Alls I had to do was dangle something over his head, and he would stare at it for hours. Like, really. For hours.

I always say that once a kid learns to roll over, it's like they take this Asshole Pill. Suddenly, they're into everything. Fingers go in closing doors. Rubber bands go around cupboard knobs to keep those munchkins out of there. Johnny did that, but months ahead of other babies. You'd blink and find him crawling behind the toilet. His motor skills changed so fast and were so damned sharp, I thought I had a baby genius.

I'm not sure when I figured out he's different from all the others. I'm not sure if it was his humming while he climbs shelves and such, or the fact he never looks me in the eye. Most likely, it was the fact I have to catch him immediately after pooping and change him, otherwise he spreads it on the walls, laughing. It calms him down or something. No matter how many time-outs and talking-tos I give him, next poop there he is, streaking it along the hallway. I mean, do you understand how hard I have to squeeze him between my legs to keep him still, while I chip away at shit under his fingernails? And do you understand the looks I get from the people at Food Basics, wondering why I am yet again buying bleach? It's why I can't leave him with Mr George. The old man can barely stand, so Sylvie is enough for him. And he is a hefty boy. The only person athletic enough to play with him was Victor, that Black boy who lived in our old complex. When he got arrested (for nothing at all, mind you), and after we were transferred to the Galloway Shelter, Johnny was so sad not to be climbing the length of Victor each morning.

To be honest, Johnny's ways give me knots in my stomach. Like, I am worried that if I tell somebody about it, somebody like a social worker or a teacher, someone will take my kids away. Or if I try to get help, I couldn't afford it. And in between, I get these stares from people, like he's a freak.

"How old is he?" I hate this question. This was from a group of white ladies who bring their kids into the literacy centre.

"He's three."

"Wow, he is one big boy," said Fern, who is a stay-at-home mom.

Helen chimed in. She is an auntie taking care of her kin. "Yeah, I was going to say! He's pretty big. He must be a handful!"

I could tell they were fishing. Fern leaned in. "He seems, you know ... pretty big, but he's ..." I kept silent.

Helen nervously added, "Does he ... you know ... speak much?"

They each took a slow and thoughtful swig of their Starbucks coffee and looked at me, feigning concern.

"He's more of a climber."

They both groaned in agreement and chuckled. "Well, we can see that!" Fern shot Helen a look.

When I didn't give them the information they wanted, they closed their circle. With their backs to me, they talked about random shit, like carpet restoration and catering companies. Every now and then one of them would turn to me with a half-hearted smile and try to involve me in their conversation.

"Well, you know what it's like, trying to do that long drive to cottage country on a Friday afternoon!"

Umm. No, I do not. Nor will I, ever. Fern knows full well, looking at my second-hand clothes—this goddamn Canada T-shirt with the name "Sarah" marked on the label and these tear-away pants— that I have never been to any cottage, thank you very much.

I was glad for Ms Hina. I could tell by the way she positioned her shoulders that she, too, was drowning them out. Plus, I know she has a special place in her heart for Johnny. She knows things aren't quite the same for him.

One of Johnny's favourite things to do is turn lights on and off. The look on his face is priceless. The wonder of it all. One direction, there is light. Another direction, there is darkness. One day at the literacy centre, Johnny wouldn't leave the switch alone. Humming as he usually does, he climbed the bookshelves to get to the light switch and began his on-off routine. I didn't mind it so much, as it kept him from eating the playdough. I was also busy sweeping up the sand off the floors.

All of a sudden, that bitch Helen picked Johnny up under the arms, sat him down, and screamed at him while wagging her finger, "It's cleanup time!"

I was mortified. Really and truly, my heart stopped. I know this.

He was so far away from me, everyone surrounding him like he was to be hanged. And he kept humming. I'm going to be honest, there was a part of me that wondered if this was right. It's my own stuff, you know. Thinking that way. Like it's bad to be different. I felt my voice rising though, to its rightful place, out loud, into the air for everyone to hear.

"Get away from him now!" I said firmly. I had never heard myself like that before. Loud enough that my ears were ringing. My cheeks were red and hot. You could have fried an egg on my forehead. "He is not like your kids. You get away from him."

Ms Hina stopped slicing oranges. She entered the scene wiping her hands with a brown paper towel.

"Is everything okay?" she asked.

"These women think he's bad, but Johnny isn't a bad boy, you understand?"

Helen began treading backwards, not making eye contact. "I wasn't saying—"

"Never *ever* touch him again. Johnny is different. He doesn't even know how to stop himself for anything. He has different needs. He isn't hurting anyone." And that's when Johnny came up to me and bit my hand. I must have scared him with my yelling. It certainly wasn't the first time he'd bitten me. He had done it so many times, my skin was practically rubber. But this time, I was so hyped up and ready to fight that I let out a squeal. I shook my hand and checked for blood. Only teeth marks. I quickly grabbed Johnny and hugged him. I stroked his hair and kissed his forehead.

The group of women huddled together, silenced and embarrassed. I made a point to stay a bit longer, not moving a single inch until they all left, to ensure they wouldn't think I was scared by their presence. I let Johnny turn the lights on and off. Eventually, Ms Hina took her room keys off the wall for Johnny to play with, because she knew he loved all things metal.

As soon as those ladies went about their quiet privileged lives, I put Johnny in his stroller and let him play with my wedding ring until he fell asleep. I pulled up one of those tiny kid-sized chairs and stared at him. Ms Hina pulled up a chair beside me. We both looked so funny with our knees close to our chins. But we didn't feel like laughing.

"Hey, Marie. Would you be open to talking while Johnny is asleep?"

I nodded. I just wanted to hear the words.

"I want you to know that I am speaking with you now and that it's not bad news. I just want to help you. Would you be open to that?"

The tears rolling down my face cooled everything down. I was reminded of those old Pepsi cans from the eighties with the two holes: one for drinking from, the other just to relieve the pressure in the can. That was me, decompressing.

"I have been watching Johnny for a while. He is an amazing kid. But I can see he is finding it challenging to express what he wants or to look anyone in the eye. Now, I'm not an expert. But I think it would be beneficial to get him assessed by one. Once we have that assessment, and if they determine that Johnny needs to learn differently, then we can work together to find the right services for him.

Does that sound like something you would be interested in?"

It was like I was peeing from my face. The tears kept coming and coming. I sounded like I was choking on a carrot. I had to stifle myself so's not to wake Johnny up.

"The doctor at the walk-in clinic didn't want him to get assessed."

Ms Hina grabbed a box of tissues off the windowsill and offered it to me. I wiped my face.

"Since he's too young for school, you actually need to see a family doctor. The walk-in clinic should have told you that. I'm sorry they gave you the wrong information. It's a family doctor who refers you to a behavioural psychologist to assess him."

"I don't have a family doctor."

"We'll get you one."

"But a family doctor's hours ... I have to be here by the time school ends ..."

"I know. All of these challenges are completely valid. But I will try my best to help you."

After Ms Hina closed up shop at the centre, I walked with Johnny in the stroller. I walked and walked until I realized the shoelaces on my soggy running shoes were untied. I walked until it was time to pick up Sylvie at school.

It didn't matter. Those ladies didn't matter. I was going to understand him. His special language.

Ms Hina managed to find me a family doctor at East York Hospital. It was so far away, but she drove us to our appointment after centre hours.

While she was unbuckling Johnny from a borrowed car seat she said, "It's probably best we don't share this with anyone at the centre, okay?"

The family doctor happened to be a high school friend of Ms Hina's. She also wore a hijab. Ms Hina explained the situation after I filled out the paperwork to be one of this doctor's patients. The doctor began typing on her laptop, then printed out the referral to a behavioural psychologist. It felt like that golden ticket in *Charlie and the Chocolate Factory*.

The next morning, Michelle, the shelter supervisor, approached me in the hallway as we were on our way to drop Sylvie off at school.

"Hi, Michelle!" said Sylvie.

"Hey, sweet girl," Michelle turned to me with a note. "It's a message for you."

I looked at the pink chit of paper. It read, "Dr Berger. Appointment set for November 10, 1:00 p.m., West Hill Memorial Hospital, Child Development Clinic."

"That's a month from now," I whispered under my breath. I tried to catch Michelle as she was walking away. "Hey, Michelle. Sorry to bother you, but I'll need some more tokens for the bus, please."

On the day of the assessment, not only did Johnny decide to pick his nose until it bled, but there was a transit strike. I dropped Sylvie off at school, then walked Johnny in his stroller, blood all over his face, straight to the literacy centre.

"Psst," Ms Hina gestured for me to go to a corner of the centre and secretly handed me a fifty-dollar bill.

"I can't accept that!"

"Yes, you can. There's a transit strike. You need to get to an appointment you've been waiting a month for. There is blood all over your child's face. You still need to get back here in time for Sylvie after school. You can accept this money. Take a cab." She straightened her hijab and looked around conspiratorially. "Plus, I need to reimburse you for cooking the community meal this week, *remember*?"

Of course, I didn't remember. God bless that woman's soul.

The specialist's office was exactly how I pictured it in my head. We were ushered into a room with a small table and chairs. On the table were three large balls of green, blue, and pink playdough. Next to them sat a basket of blocks. Dr Berger, this white lady with red curly hair, asked me to take Johnny out of the stroller. Johnny went straight to the light switch on the wall. He reached his hand up and could not touch it. So he pulled a chair to the wall and stood on top of it. Now his hand reached it; he turned the light on and off. On and off. Over and over he did this, while Dr Berger asked questions both to me and to Johnny.

She asked me to leave the room for a moment. I sat in another room with a TV screen where I could watch what was happening. Johnny began screaming as soon as I left. He didn't want to engage in any of the activities. He began hitting his own head with his fists. He tried to bite Dr Berger. The doctor smiled up at the camera, pretending to be calm.

"Miss Beaudoin, can you come back inside?" At first I was embarrassed but then reminded myself that she must have seen this kind of stuff a million times. I came back inside the room, and Johnny ran to my leg.

"Can I put him back in the stroller?"

"Absolutely."

"It's time for his nap anyway." I strapped him in, and I let him play with my wedding ring as he usually did until he fell asleep.

Dr Berger kept smiling. I kept thinking about how Ms Hina said this wasn't bad news. It helped me a lot, remembering that nothing this lady was going to say was bad news.

"So, Miss Beaudoin, I have some observations about Johnny. Are you open to hearing them?"

"I've been open for a long time, doctor."

She smiled. This was not bad news.

"Good. From what I can see here, Johnny has autistic disorder, operating at a twelve-month capacity despite being three years old. It's important to give him this designation because then you will have access to programs that will help him."

"That's what we need. Thank you, doctor."

"I understand your housing is precarious at the moment?"

If precarious meant we lived in a place where you needed to get buzzed in by twenty-four-hour staff because the other occupants were being chased by either their abusive partners or their angry drug dealers, then yes, it was precarious indeed.

"When you see my receptionist at the front, she will give you a list of free resources and specialists. I'm going to warn you though. This is not going to be easy. These resources might be hard to get to. They're far apart from each other, and often times you will be given only a limited number of sessions per specialist. There are usually long waiting lists for these services. A lot of this work has to be done at home, and I can't even imagine how difficult that will be, given you don't even have a secure home." She touched my shoulder gently. "Are you ready for this challenge?"

I did go from service to service trying to find support, sometimes through snowstorms, using my ugly twenty-dollar stroller with a kid as large as Johnny in it, that damned thing with its crooked wheels making crooked lines through the slush. I knocked on office doors. Found doors locked after I had just missed appointments because of a transit delay. Cried in hallways. On the days I miraculously made it to appointments, I was told not to expect him to ever be toilet trained. I was told not to expect him to ever use full sentences. I was told to start planning on what his support structure would look like when I was an old lady, unable to cart around an adult in diapers. I didn't care about all of that. I just wanted to understand him. His own special language.

The speech therapist—with whom I had a whopping six sessions—gave me a binder full of laminated pages of cartoon images. Some of the images illustrated faces with emotions. Some images illustrated food. Some were of toys, and some were of activities. Since Johnny was motivated by food, the therapist placed apple slices on the table.

"Apple." She pointed to the apple. She pointed to the cartoon image on the laminated page. "Apple." This went on for thirty minutes, until Johnny decided to poop his pants.

After those six sessions were over—all located an hour-and-a-half west of our shelter, mind you—the only thing Johnny learned was that shitting himself quickly ended the session.

"Just have patience, Miss Beaudoin," the speech therapist told me. "Sometimes this can take months and months."

"But I only had you for six sessions."

I was showing Sylvie how to floss her teeth one night. Poor thing has been so neglected. With everything happening to Johnny, I just about left her high and dry.

"It's bleeding!"

"How do you know? You got eyes inside your mouth?" She struggled to get herself free from my prying thumbs. There was just one little piece of corn there, way in the back.

"I can taste it, Mama! Stop!"

I stopped. There was blood. I felt like a right asshole looking at the blood staining poor Sylvie's pyjama collar. I could have told her I'd never let her eat corn again if this drama continues, or something motherly like that, but I think we both had had enough. I washed her face and kissed her chin and cheeks, seeing as I couldn't kiss her gums.

I tucked her in, just the way she likes it. Two pillows on either side, blanket to the chin.

"Want to hear a story?" I asked her while stroking her hair away from her face.

She nodded yes. She loved to be touched.

I told her the story of my grandma and how she was a teacher. Her trailer was next to a lead, zinc, and copper mine in New Brunswick. She taught reading to the miners.

"What? They can't read?" I asked her, laughing at the thought of a helpless adult. I was a smart-ass child.

"Oh yeah, sure. These men, they all got through school without teachers even knowing if they were literate. They didn't care. Not when they were destined for deep elevators and pickaxes."

I would sit beside my grandma and watch her teach these men, belittled and eating humble pie with every new word in English or French. She would kick me under the table if I tried to beat the student to the punch.

"They're already embarrassed. They don't need any reminding from you, dear."

One night, the lesson with her usual student, Ben, was interrupted by his wife, Rita. She came in with her chin up, saying she was "just in to pick up Ben," then took a seat on my grandma's couch.

"Did you notice that lady? Did you see her putting on airs, like she could read herself?" my grandma said. "She brought a newspaper just to show me how. But when you have taught for as long as I have, you know when people are just looking at the pictures."

Sylvie was listening hard to my story. Then she shook her arms out of the covers I had tucked under her. She held my face like she always does when she wants my undivided attention. "Maybe Rita wanted to learn how to read, too. She wanted to learn but was too ashamed."

There is something about that memory that gives me hope. So much hope that even after I watched Sylvie fall asleep and turned out the lights, I stared out the window until the streetlamp became blurry.

The next day there was a snowstorm. I didn't give a shit. I fed Johnny and Sylvie hot oatmeal. After I dropped Sylvie off at school, I walked as fast as I could in my squishy sneakers to the library.

Johnny was asleep and blanketed in his stroller. I used the computer and looked up anything about communication with people who
have autism. I didn't even take off my coat. I was soggy but deter-
mined. It was hilarious, at first, thinking of how good a drinking
game it would be to down a shot every time I watched another video
of a researcher showing a brain lit up by animated bolts of lightning.
Yes, I know, I thought to myself. My child is so disorderly and such a
mystery. It was sickening.

I found this one video of these kids with autism using tablets to
communicate their basic needs. Same thing as my laminated pages,
but with these fancy tablet things. This little boy, around Johnny's
age, tapped away at images on this tablet to tell his caregiver he needed a drink, or wanted to play. I watched as many videos as I could to
see how the therapists taught the kids. I looked at Johnny, asleep in
the stroller. I put the rain cover on the stroller and headed out again
into the snow to the literacy centre. I was going to do it myself.

I entered the centre, and those damn ladies with their Starbucks
coffees took one look at me and my snow-drenched hair and began
convening in the far corner. I didn't care. I was on a mission.

I wanted to add images that Johnny recognized to the book. I
also thought he might have a better chance if they were actual photos
and not drawings. Ms Hina supplied me with the magazine clippings,
construction paper, glue, scissors, and markers. She even offered
me a hole punch and binder. I found actual photos of things I knew
Johnny liked. A kid biting into an apple. A tray full of crackers. A
woman drinking a glass of milk. A little boy playing with trains. A
man fixing a light switch. An ad showing a woman using keys in a

door lock. Anything I could think of. I started with ten squares of images at first.

Edna helped me cut the squares and arrange them in the binder.

"Did you want me to laminate them as well?" Ms Hina asked.

"I dunno." I looked at Johnny, full of doubt. "This may not work."

Edna slapped my shoulder playfully, the way she always does. "It will work! Have faith." Damn Catholics.

I waited until it was snack time at the literacy centre. I turned the page to "Apple," with a big picture of an apple on it.

"Johnny," I said to him while hooking my finger around a chunk of playdough in his mouth and throwing it in the garbage. "Do you want apple?" I pointed at the picture. "Apple?" I had a slice of apple in my hand at the ready. Hopeful. Scared.

Johnny stared at it for a long time. Then he walked away. My heart dropped. Why did I think this was a good idea?

Ms Hina rubbed my shoulder reassuringly. "It may take some time."

I cut the apple into smaller slices. I put them in my pocket.

"Johnny, look. Look. Apple." I pointed at the picture. He stopped humming. I took his hand and touched it to the picture. "Apple." I handed him one piece of the apple and he swiped it away and onto the floor. I did this four more times, until all the apple pieces were gone. What a waste.

Ms Hina encouraged me to do this again and again at every snack time, since Johnny loves eating. I should know; I'm the one cleaning the shit that exits him each time he eats!

After about three months of this apple nonsense, I was about to give up. Maybe it had to be a tablet, like in the video. Not a bunch of cut-up pictures in a binder. Maybe the lamination on the pictures made it too shiny for him to read. I was feeling lost and sad.

"Now you're a teacher, Mama," Sylvie said to me while I was tucking her in.

"What do you mean, missy poops?"

"You're teaching Johnny how to speak using that book."

It broke my heart to think the book might not work.

One morning it was warm enough that we could hear the snow thawing. The snow was turning to water again under our feet. The mud ran past my sneakers, like a promise.

"Can you hear that, Johnny?" I asked him while he kicked his legs happily in his stroller. We saw some pigeons up ahead eating grain on the melting ice. Pushing the stroller ahead of me like a toboggan, I ran and slid along the ice to scare them. Up the pigeons flew, and Johnny squealed in delight. It made me so happy to hear his laugh.

We went into the literacy centre, just in time for snack. Edna was there that day and gave me a hug. Ms Hina gave me a handful of apple.

I sat down in one of those goddamn kid's chairs, with my knees almost up to my ears. I placed the binder in my lap and opened it to the picture of the apple. "Apple? Do you want an apple?" I said to Johnny. I took his hand, touched the picture, and gave him an apple. Same thing as ever. No difference. I was no expert. Who was I to think this could work? I got up to stretch my legs, and the binder fell to the floor. It opened to the picture of crackers.

Johnny stopped humming and put his hand on the picture. Ms Hina and I stared at each other, then we looked at Johnny.

"Johnny? Crackers? Do you want crackers?"

I waved my hand at Edna, and she ran to grab the crackers from the cupboard and placed them in my hand.

"Crackers?" I put Johnny's hand on the crackers. He looked at my handful of crackers, then placed his hand on the picture. He pointed at it. He pointed at the goddamn picture.

I handed him a cracker, and he ate it. He pointed at the goddamn picture and got what he wanted. All this time, he didn't really want an apple. He just wanted a cracker.

I picked him up so hard, he almost lost his cracker.

"Cracker! Cracker!" I cried while dancing in a circle. Ms Hina went to the classroom cupboard and took out a sleeve of crackers. She was jumping, too.

"Cracker! Cracker!" we sang. Those snooty white ladies were silent, wondering what the hell was going on.

With Johnny in my arms, his mouth full of mush and drool, I ran up the stairs to Sylvie's classroom. Mrs Finnegan was pouring glue into egg cartons.

"She's not here right now. She should be in French class. Is everything alright?"

"Everything is great!" I was already out the door, trying to find Madame Gauthier's class.

I followed the sound of the singsong French.

"Je soo-wee. Tooo ehhhh. Eeeel ehhhh."

I barged into the room like a giant was about to attack the school.

"Je m'excuse!" I said to the teacher, then turned to Sylvie. Poor thing thought somebody died or something. I knelt down and kissed her forehead, Johnny still wrapped around me like a monkey. "He pointed at the picture of the cracker, and he got a cracker!"

Sylvie and I began dancing around Johnny, laughing and crying. "Cracker! Cracker!"

PART 4

SUMMER

The mayflies have come early this year, making the Rouge River hum and sing into a new season. Grandfather Heron is back, watching from his post amidst the reeds.

At the corner of Orton Park and Ellesmere Road
Car windows are rolled down and the volume turned up. Rear-view mirrors shake with the reverberations of a season arrived.

At Victoria Park and Danforth Avenues
Five smiling women are holding certificates. They have completed a program for teaching computer skills to survivors of domestic abuse. They pose for a picture, then hug each other tightly. A new beginning.

DAILY REPORT

June 28, 2012

Facilitator: Hina Hassani

Location: Rouge Hill Public School

Attendance:

Parent/Guardian/Caregiver	Children (one per line please)
Marie Beaudoin	Sylvie Beaudoin
	Johnny Beaudoin
Edna Espiritu	Bernard Espiritu
Helen McKay	Finnegan Everson
	Liam Williams
Fern Donahue	Paulo Sanchez
	Kyle Keegan
Natalia Angelo	Marca Angelo
Pamela Roy	Evan Roy
	Yanna Roy
	Tasha Roy

Notes:

   Today we baked a vanilla chocolate chip cake for Bing's goodbye party. Our little genius is off and away to the gifted program next year! It was very difficult, as you can imagine, to get the toddlers to place the chocolate chips into the batter instead of eating them right out of the bag. I'm not sure how we even ended up with a finished product, but we did. Bing was so very happy.

Tomorrow I'm thinking we will do our graduation ceremony for all our school-aged children. I know it's risky to have sweets two days in a row, but why not? It's the end of the school year. Rainbow cupcakes it is! No supplies needed this time around, as you know, and I will begin prep for cleaning once school is out. By tomorrow, I will start to give away the rest of our perishable groceries.

I have touched base with Tammy over at East Side Early Play, and we are very excited to begin planning out activities for September. Now that we have daily access to their gym, we can finally incorporate more movement, dance, and games. Tammy has a yoga background, and I have a dance background, so it's kind of perfect. I have informed the parents at Rouge Hill Public School of the change. Some are thrilled about it; some are not so thrilled. But the general consensus is that the bus stop right outside the main entrance is a real winner. Thank you for keeping me amongst the community I have learned to love.

Have a wonderful summer, Evalyn.

SYLVIE

"If there are any dancers out there, please report to the east doors of the school," said the voice on the loud speaker.

We pow wow dancers shuffled through the grounds of Rouge Hill Public School—from the ice cream truck to the policeman on horseback; from the drummer's tent to the taco stand—but never to the east doors of the school, as instructed.

It was a hot day for the Scarborough East Pow Wow. The sun blazed through rainbows of ribbon. The sun blazed through tightly bound braids upon scalps wet with sweat. Through metal cones on jingle dresses. Through feathered bustles and fancy shawls.

Everywhere I went, I could hear visitors yelp when they sat on the burning hot plastic seats to wait for the Grand Entry.

"Hot, eh?"

"Isn't it ever."

"When are those dancers going to start?"

"I dunno."

Bing and I sat under a skinny tree much too young to give shade. It was difficult to strike a balance between crouching close enough to share relief from the hot sun and not touching so that we could avoid each other's body heat. So we tried to cool ourselves with ice cream instead, bugging our mamas at regular intervals for pocket change.

I struggled to keep my ice cream upright while my jingle dress cones hung downwards catching on the grass. Bing, of course, expertly bit into his ice cream, consuming it without drips or dribbles.

"Please, folks, we want to get started on the Grand Entry. Please, if you are a dancer, make your way to the east doors of the school."

"Aren't you a dancer?" Bing said, pretending to be responsible.

"Yup," I said, licking melted chocolate ice cream off my wrists.

I looked around the yard and laughed. Kids everywhere in their regalia, at odds with their parents. Sour cream smeared across moccasins. Headdresses crooked on top of tiny toddler heads. "If Mommy gives you one more cookie, will you stop pulling on your braids?!" I heard a mom say to her daughter whose hair had gone undone and fuzzy. "Will you sit down? The Grand Entry is about to start!"

I could see Elder Fay take her place at the beginning of the procession. Her wrinkly face squinted at the hot sun while she positioned her shawl over her left arm and her feather fan in her right hand. I gobbled up my ice cream and took my place behind her and the other elders and behind the veterans holding flags. Mama rushed over with a baby wipe to clean my chocolate-covered face.

I thought it was the sight of Levy, that very serious boy, in his grass dancing regalia and child-sized feather buttress that had Mama holding back tears. But when she held my cheeks after wiping them, I realized she was crying at the sight of me.

"You're beautiful, Sylvie." I blushed. I had never heard that before.

Mama hurried back to her picnic blanket, where Johnny and Bing's mom were sitting, to watch the Grand Entry finally begin. Johnny, who was in his stroller sucking the sleeves of his ribbon shirt, suddenly sat up at the sound of the drumming.

"Look! It's your sister, Johnny!" Mama pointing at me, my hands at my waist, bouncing at the knees, and following the procession.

The procession made its way around the circle to the other end, where Mama was sitting. She was still crying. I waved my arms at her to join me. Mama shook her head no. I waved again. Bing's mom elbowed Mama in the ribs, until Mama finally stood.

Mama wiped away her tears. "I don't know. I don't think I earned this dance." I said nothing. I just held her hand in mine, rubbing the back of it with my thumb. We both automatically put our free hands to our waists and began dancing.

The procession continued in a circle to the tune of men wailing, each of them drumming with one hand and the other hand covering an ear. Wee children in their fancy shawls turned circles around each other. Levy's dance looked like he was having a conversation with the ground. Edna stayed with Johnny, who cheered at the sight of us, ribbons still in his mouth.

From afar, I could see Bing watching from under our skinny tree. He waved. Just then, there was a fierce wind. It cooled all of us down. I knew it was time. As the procession moved away, I waved goodbye, and I looked forward.

LAURA

I am standing just close enough to Mrs Kamal, until she begins to speak to me. She thinks I am the spirit of her dead brother. But I'm not. I'm Laura. I try to tell her it's me, the girl from across the hall. I want to say thank you for feeding me when Mommy wasn't there. I want to say I know it wasn't her who kicked me out of her house once she found lice in my hair. That it was her husband who wanted me to go. So, as a favour, I stand here so she can speak to her dead brother like he's here. I want to say he's off near that river where they used to skip rocks, but I think she wants to believe he's here beside her. It's not that he doesn't care. It's just that he's happier there. And he loves to skip rocks. He showed me once how he can make the rocks jump, not once but hundreds of times. He held up a smooth, flat rock, his secret to being so good at it. Then he pointed to the wound on his arm. So that's how he left, I figured.

Mrs Kamal always waits until no one is around, then begins to speak to me in her language. Sometimes she laughs. Sometimes she sits for a long time, looking out in the distance. Today, she is sitting in her section of the Galloway Park community garden. We can both hear the sound of the drums at the pow wow. She frowns in the direction of the noise. She doesn't like those people. She says something I can't hear. Shakes her head and takes away the dead leaves from her vegetable patch. I have watched her grow it since I left and the weather became warmer. This is where she talks to me the most. I have watched her peel open wet toilet paper rolls with tiny seedlings growing inside. I have watched green sprouts come out of the dirt and watched her grab some of them and place them in her mouth. She says in her language something about it tasting so good. I can tell, the way she closes her eyes and makes noises.

Without any gloves on, she uses her hands to turn the dirt until it's all dark again. I wish I could help her. I wish I could taste those sprouts, too. Once she is done with the dirt, she stands up and cracks her back. Her hands are on her bum, and she bends backwards. She makes a noise. She almost forgets to put water on the vegetables and I whisper to her to feed them. She listens. She sinks a white cup into a big bucket full of water and feeds every vegetable, like we're at dinner. Like each vegetable is over for dinner, and she's giving them each a glass of beer. I laugh a bit. She stops. I cover my mouth.

Mrs Kamal finds a tree stump to sit on. She knows I am following her as she sits down. She says his name. Youssef? Youssef? She knows now. It's not him. She looks in my direction, even though she can't see me and I can't answer. She covers her mouth and cries. I put my hand on her shoulder and she cries even more. I try to show her the rocks skipping, to make her stop. That's when the wind begins to pick up and shake all the trees.

The trees dance. The plants and flowers dance. Mrs Kamal holds her hijab down. The wind is so strong. I can't even hear Mrs Kamal crying anymore. I can just hear the wind.

"Why won't you leave?" says the wind.

I don't know what to say. I've never spoken to the wind before. I haven't been spoken to since I left. So I stay quiet. The wind picks up and nearly sweeps me up and away like a balloon.

"Why are you here?"

"Because ..." I think real hard. I put my hand on my heart. "Because I don't want her to cry."

"She won't cry forever." The wind sounds like leaves clapping.

"How do you know? I've seen her cry for so long."

"She won't cry forever."

"What about everyone else? How can I leave?"

"If I tell you that if you let go, you can see that no one cries forever, will you leave?"

"And go where?"

"You know where. Youssef is already there, skipping rocks."

The wind makes a circle around Mrs Kamal. A circle of dust. I see her there crying. I know if I stay, she will cry more. I say yes.

I watch Mrs Kamal wipe her tears away. She picks up a dandelion wish and looks at it. She closes her eyes to say goodbye to Youssef and blows. The wishes float into the air, and I watch them. One of the wishes grows and grows until it is large enough to take me by the hand. The wind laughs, probably because I'm making a face, I'm so scared to fly. But I am. I am flying.

Mrs Kamal multiplies into millions of beads, like her necklace—it is a necklace of Mrs Kamals. I follow the beads and can see her face growing older, no longer crying. She is kissing her children's foreheads goodnight. She is making food and smiling, harvesting her vegetables and watching the sunset. She grows older and older. She is blowing out candles, being helped up and down the stairs. Old and wrinkly, she is kissed on the forehead by her children. She dies smiling. She meets Youssef at the river again. He has a pile of smooth, flat rocks to show her.

I see a necklace of Ms Hinas. I see her sitting beside piles and piles of paper with hundreds and hundreds of children's names on them. Her brown hands look at each page and remember each child. I see her holding close to her heart the picture I drew for her. She saves my picture and places the rest in recycling. She closes the doors to the centre one last time.

I see a necklace of Bings. I see him running to another man in an airport. He is older and older. He is sitting beside his mom, holding her hands while she says goodbye. He cries, loud. He almost leaves that man he ran to at the airport. But he decides to stay, because he loves him.

I see a necklace of Sylvies. I see her writing and writing. I see her stories being read by so many people. I see her being sad sometimes because she misses her dad. She is smoking by the water. Sometimes she thinks of me. When she is done smoking, she goes back inside her house to write some more, and she feels better.

I follow the necklaces, up and up and up and up and up, past the trees, until everyone looks like ants. I follow these necklaces, people I have never seen. People I have only dreamt of. I follow the necklaces into the clouds, until I can no longer hear the wind. All I can hear is quiet. It is darker now. The sky is pink. The air is warm. I can hear myself breathing. What do I do now?

I hear my name. Laura. I turn toward the darkest part of the sky. I can see stars.

"Daddy?"

He stands there. Afraid of me but smiling. He wonders if I am angry. His skin is pink. His hair is clean. He wears a T-shirt and jeans; his hands are in his pockets.

When you're dead, you can't tell someone, "You will change your ways," because their ways won't continue ever again. But my daddy. My daddy takes off his shirt. I see he has no tattoos or scars. Just him. He shakes his shirt. From it comes millions and millions of stars, flying into the sky and taking their places. Twinkling stars. I laugh. He laughs too.

He puts his shirt back on. He reaches into his pocket and pulls out darkness. He spreads it around the stars to make them twinkle even brighter. He opens his arms and asks if I would like a hug. I walk to him. I'm so scared. But then he holds me. He smells like food. He smells like flowers. And smiles. And sorrys. And If Onlys. I Never Meant Tos. I'm Different Nows. I've Learned So Muches. I'm Not the Sames. I've never been hugged like that before, and that hug feels so good, so I hug him back. It feels so good to hug someone who will never hit you.

Below us, a bunch of geese fly like an arrow toward the sunset. The sky gets darker. I ask him what happens now. He doesn't answer. He just holds me tight, smelling like home.

Acknowledgments

Salamat sa'inyong lahat.

This novel is about community. Thank you to the community who helped make this novel possible. I fully acknowledge the privilege I hold in this world and cannot be more grateful to the countless people who checked my work for cultural references. Your time and knowledge was appreciated. Thank you to the Toronto Zoo for letting me conduct orangutan research on site. To the beautiful people of Scarborough and all of the people who privately interviewed with me about their lives: thank you for inspiring me with your resilience and strength. To my east side mamas, Rashida, Meaghan, Victoria, and Jen, and to my beautiful Hernandez/Estioko family: thank you for believing in each page. To my mother, Cecille Estioko Hernandez: thank you for your expert translation. To Rania El Mugammar and Starr Domingue for their time and patience educating me. To the Scarborough Arts Council, Ontario Arts Council, and Diaspora Dialogues: thank you for the funding and support your organizations have given me throughout my career. To Jim Wong-Chu and all the wonderful people behind the Asian Canadian Writers' Workshop: the mentorship you gave me was priceless. To Charm Torres, Zahra Siddiqui, Annie Gibson, S. Bear Bergman, and Michael Erickson: thank you for being generous when I had little to give. To Donna-Michelle St. Bernard: I am honoured to have received your guidance. To the amazing Team Arsenal Pulp Press: thank you for believing in this first-time writer, pushing me hard, and knowing I can make magic with words. To Arden McNeilly, who helped me copyedit my manuscript: I am an artist because you are my daughter. To my partner, Nazbah Tom: thank you for hearing me read every damn draft of my novel and cheering me on. To M——: your memory burns brighter than your final moments. I am wishing you rivers and quiet wherever you are.

photo: Yeemi Tang

Catherine Hernandez is a queer theatre practitioner and writer. Her plays *Singkil* and *Kilt Pins* were published by Playwrights Canada Press. Her children's book *M is for Mustache: A Pride ABC Book* was published by Flamingo Rampant. She is the Artistic Director of Sulong Theatre for women of colour. She lives in Scarborough, Ontario.

catherinehernandezcreates.com